Bolan stare
in the crac

His Arab makeup was long gone, washed away by blood and abuse. The swelling had gone down somewhat, but he could still barely recognize himself.

Methodically he set about cleaning and dressing their wounds, working on Johnny first.

"Where do you go from here, Mack?" his brother asked as Bolan bandaged a long cut on Johnny's arm. The word "you" was not lost on Bolan.

"Jerusalem," he said.

"What's there?"

"The old city," Bolan replied. "King David's city. Abba and his . . . associates are going to blow up the Wailing Wall tonight."

"What? You must tell someone about this, Mack."

"No!" Bolan said vehemently. "Abba's mine."

MACK BOLAN

The Executioner

DON PENDLETON's EXECUTIONER

MACK BOLAN

Death Has a Name

A GOLD EAGLE BOOK FROM

W⦿RLDWIDE

TORONTO • NEW YORK • LONDON • PARIS
AMSTERDAM • STOCKHOLM • HAMBURG
ATHENS • MILAN • TOKYO • SYDNEY

First edition December 1986

ISBN 0-373-61096-3

Special thanks and acknowledgment to
Mike McQuay for his contributions to this work.

Printed in Canada

Now this is the Law of the Jungle—as old and as
  true as the sky;
And the Wolf that shall keep it may prosper, but the
  Wolf that shall break it must die.

> —Rudyard Kipling, *The Law of the Jungle*

The wolves are gathering. Let us watch and wait.

> —Mack Bolan

THE
MACK BOLAN
LEGEND

Nothing less than a war could have fashioned the destiny of the man called Mack Bolan. Bolan earned the Executioner title in the jungle hellgrounds of Vietnam, for his skills as a crack sniper in pursuit of the enemy.

But this supreme soldier also wore another name—Sergeant Mercy. He was so tagged because of the compassion he showed to wounded comrades-in-arms and Vietnamese civilians.

Mack Bolan's second tour of duty ended prematurely when he was given emergency leave to return home and bury his family. Bolan made his peace at his parents' and sister's gravesite. Then he declared war on the evil force that had snatched his loved ones. The Mafia.

In a fiery one-man assault, he confronted the Mob head-on, carrying a cleansing flame to the urban menace. And when the battle smoke cleared, a solitary figure walked away alive.

He continued his lone-wolf struggle, and soon a hope of victory began to appear. But Mack Bolan had broken society's every rule. That same society started gunning for this elusive warrior—to no avail.

So Bolan was offered amnesty to work within the system against international terrorism. This time, as an official employee of Uncle Sam, Bolan wore yet another handle: Colonel John Phoenix. With government sanction now, and a command center at Stony Man Farm in Virginia's Blue Ridge Mountains, he and his new allies—Able Team and Phoenix Force—waged relentless war on a new adversary: the KGB and all it stood for.

Until the inevitable occurred. Bolan's one true love, the brilliant and beautiful April Rose, died at the hands of the Soviet terror machine.

Embittered and utterly saddened by this feral deed, Bolan broke the shackles of Establishment authority.

Now the big justice fighter is once more free to haunt the treacherous alleys of the shadow world.

1

The Executioner felt his hands tighten on the choir loft railing as the organ strains of the wedding march floated hollowly through the high vaulted ceiling of the old Catholic church. From his vantage point, he looked down and saw Tomasso "Big Tommy" Metrano walking slowly down the center aisle in a black tux, his daughter gliding gently beside him, the train of her long white lace gown being carried by two little girls no older than six.

The group moved toward the altar, toward the priest and shiny-faced altar boys, toward the young man with bright eyes who waited to take Carla Metrano from the arm of her infamous father.

The Executioner was the name he used, but Mack Bolan was the name he had been born with—and it was Bolan who felt the growing tightness in his chest. It was all wrong here.

Despite the Mafia button who lay unconscious beside him in the loft, his hands still clutching a Wilkinson "Terry" carbine, Bolan knew it couldn't go here. There was innocence mixed with the incense and the organ music that kept him from snuffing Big Tommy right on the spot.

He had been on Metrano's trail for months, cutting a bloody swath through the capo's loan-sharking, dope and flesh empire that stretched from Seattle all the way here to West Palm Beach, Florida. But Metrano had eluded the Executioner—and the rightful death that awaited the mafioso. He kept himself hidden from public view, his personal security all but unbreachable. Except here, at his daughter's wedding.

Bolan thought about Carla Metrano, and hoped that the sins of the father wouldn't touch the child. Then he thought about his own sister, whom he'd never be able to watch getting married or having a family because of people like Tomasso Metrano. He thought about his parents and the fullness of life they never experienced. And he thought, somewhat sadly, about himself. It was the church that did it; he was so out of place it startled him. Even Metrano had a bride to give away here.

All Bolan had to give away was death.

Metrano directed his daughter toward the smiling young man and stepped aside. Bolan watched, his face a grim mask, his hands white-knuckled on the rail. He could nail the scum right here. He'd never have a chance like this again. Metrano was a Family man and this was a Family affair, bodyguards standing like icons against the walls under the stations of the cross. A couple of grenades dropped into the congregation of about a hundred could probably set organized crime back twenty years. Bolan was dressed to kill, in a black skinsuit and combat harness sprouting weapons and ammo; but he couldn't do it. Not here.

He backed up a step, ready to climb out the high window and down the rope that had got him in.

Suddenly there was a commotion below, several bodyguards moving to a spot in the congregation. Bolan crept up to the rail again and looked down. They were closing in on a woman with short black hair and a white jump suit who sat among the spectators in the center of a pew. She stood, jerking her head from one side to the other. An Uzi pistol was in her hand.

Bolan's instincts took over immediately. Big Thunder was in his hand without conscious thought, the .44 AutoMag practically crying for action.

Below, the woman vaulted a pew, knocking down an old woman and a man in a walker. She jumped again, people yelling, and touched down in a crouch in the center aisle.

Everything was in motion as she sprang to her feet, stiff-arming the Uzi in front of her. There was no doubt of her target—Big Tommy.

The Uzi held a 32-round magazine of 9 mm parabellums, and it looked as if the woman intended to use every shot. The weapon bumped as she fired at Metrano, who had turned around and was moving now, but it missed, catching the priest in the shoulder instead. The slug's impact spun and sent him reeling into one of the altar boys. Big Tommy's men closed around their boss, one of them falling, then another, as they hustled the mafioso back into the sanctuary.

People ran screaming in all directions around the church as guns came out of shoulder holsters in the large hall. The .44 bucked again and again in Bolan's hand as he added his fire to the woman's, picking his targets carefully amid the insane confusion.

Gunshots echoed loudly in the cavernous church, drowning out everything else. People fell, screams lost in the wall of noise. In the aisle, the woman was hit in the thigh, a crimson stain blossoming on her pant leg. She fell behind a pew, but came up firing. Another slug took her again, high this time, in the shoulder. Then rifle fire drove Bolan back from the rail, as some of Metrano's hardmen spotted him.

And with the odds, Bolan realized it would only be a matter of time before they pinned him down. If he didn't move quickly, both he and the woman would be trapped in the church with no hope of getting out. He turned once again to the freedom of the open window behind him, then came back around.

If he had learned one thing in Nam, it was that you never left a buddy behind. And whoever the woman was, she was on his side.

Instinctively, he grabbed the rifle from the hands of the unconscious man beside him and vaulted the loft railing. He came down hard in the center aisle, falling and rolling behind a pew, rising immediately on one knee to fire down the aisle. Two men charging were picked up off their feet and thrown to the cold marble floor.

The woman was several pews ahead of him, dripping blood, valiantly keeping up the fight. He ran to her, hurdling a body that was twisted like a doll, cold eyes staring blankly, half the face missing.

He fired several times at head level, forcing people to the floor, then knelt beside the woman, her jump suit now stained completely red.

Her eyes were fluttering as she tried to speak through the pain. She was losing blood fast. Bolan grabbed her and threw her over his left shoulder, bracing the carbine under his right arm.

He started backing out of the hall, firing high, keeping them down. He heard a dull thud and felt the woman's body jerk. He knew she had been hit again.

He retreated down the aisle, an awesome figure in killer black holding a stainless-steel cannon, and made the huge archway of the door. A clutch of onlookers huddled fearfully in the atrium leading to the outside. Ignoring them, he backed out of the main doors into the hot Florida afternoon.

There was a long flight of stone steps leading up to St. Michael's. The Executioner took them sideways, always looking back the way he had come.

Two men came charging through the doorway. Bolan fired the silver hawgleg quickly, drilling them with gut hits, then the ones who followed them, the bodies hitting the steps and rolling toward, then past him.

It was a wealthy neighborhood, stately white houses with red tile roofs sitting way back behind protective walls on the palm-tree-lined streets. Bolan hurried to the line of cars parked on the street, to the black Lincoln Continental he had rented to fit in with the crowd here.

In the distance, men were pouring out of the church, laying down fire at him from the front grounds.

He jerked the door open, sliding the unconscious woman off his shoulder and into the passenger seat, pushing her head down.

Bullets zipped around him, and safety glass shattered under the onslaught of enemy fire. They were closing on him as he climbed behind the wheel and keyed the ignition. Beside him, the woman moaned loudly, partly regaining consciousness. At the end of the block, seventy feet distant, a Cadillac limo screeched around the corner and took off in the other direction. Probably Metrano, Bolan figured, trying to get away. Bolan wanted him, but the woman was his first priority now.

"Wh-who are you?" she asked weakly, her accent thick and French.

"Never mind."

"Metrano," she said, blood trickling from the corners of her mouth. "You must . . . get . . ."

"I'm getting you to a doctor," he said, pulling away from the curb, and ducking low as bullets slammed into the Lincoln.

"No!" she rasped, nearly a scream. "I will not survive. You must . . . get Metrano . . . please."

The Executioner took one look at her and knew she spoke the truth. He floored the gas pedal, sliding into the corner, and was off after Big Tommy. He stole a glance in the rearview. A convoy of Mafia crew wagons was on his tail.

2

Metrano's limo zigzagged through the wide residential streets, heading east, gunfire winking from the back windows in the blazing sunlight. Bolan swerved with it, a tough target, as neighborhood traffic climbed the curbs, churning up the manicured lawns of the stately houses. The tanks on his tail kept coming, smashing into other cars unlucky enough to be on the streets.

"Feel strong enough to shoot?" he asked the woman beside him.

She nodded painfully, grimacing, and reached for the Magnum he held out to her.

A mob soldier was leaning way out the back window of the Caddy ahead, an M-16 in his hands. He fired as they rounded a corner, missing wildly. Bolan's rental shuddered into the corner as steel-belted radials failed to grip the pavement. The heavy limo rocked on its springs as the car straightened, and Bolan saw the hardman taking aim again.

"Down!" Bolan yelled, gently but firmly pushing the woman to the seat as glass rained on them, the safety glass of the front window shattering, making vision impossible.

Bolan grabbed the rifle from the seat, using the butt to pound out the rest of the windshield. Stifling Florida air rushed in, making him squint. "Do it now," he said quietly. "Take out the son of a bitch."

The woman's face hardened. She held Big Thunder two-handed as she had the Uzi and fired methodically, the weapon kicking with each round. The man with the automatic slumped, his M-16 tumbling from his hands to dance wildly along the pavement. He lay draped through the window for a few seconds, then he was pushed out, his already dead body bouncing twice before coming to rest on a storm drain.

There was a sound in the distance, sirens. Great. More complications. The Executioner was in no better hands with the police than with the Mafia. He operated totally outside the law, hunted by his prey and by those he sought to protect. Alone, he dispensed justice the way he had been taught in the jungle, the only way he knew.

He had come back from Nam, so many years ago, to try to destroy the evil cancer of organized crime that had eaten away his family, and had perceived it to be no different from the jungles he had crawled out of. The strong and the vicious preyed on the weak, the defenseless. But when he tried to fight in this modern jungle using the techniques he had learned in the Asian hellground, he had been met with resistance and mistrust from those who stood to benefit most from his crusade.

So he fought a lonely war for the survival of civilization amid hatred and terrorism, hunted by the government he sought to protect, persecuted by the people he risked his life for.

Bolan's hand tightened on the steering wheel.

The woman coughed beside him, blood bubbling from her lips. Then the gun left weakened fingers, dropping into her lap. She slumped to the side, toward Bolan, and his right hand left the wheel to push her against her door.

"What's going on? Who are you?" he asked, skidding through another corner. The limo ahead was heading toward the bridge across the inner ocean, racing toward Palm Beach proper.

She looked at him, eyes glazing, already dead things. "Sabra," she said, more blood coming with the words. "My *plan* . . . my *plan.*"

And she was gone, all the life blasted out of her. Her head slumped on her chest, white jump suit saturated now.

Bolan was alone again.

The limo made the long stretch of drawbridge, bouncing onto it, tail end throwing sparks where metal scraped concrete. Bolan caught the rearview. Eight or ten cars were still pursuing him, the flashing lights of police cruisers weaving in and out of Mafia traffic. Big Tommy was heading home, and the Executioner had to get him before he got there.

Bolan positioned the carbine on the dash, its barrel resting on the frame of the open windshield. He triggered the weapon and scored a hit on the trunk lock. The lid flew open on the car ahead, stacks of brightly wrapped wedding presents tumbling onto the pavement.

A car slid into view abreast of him, a dark man on the passenger side leveling a sawed-off 12-gauge through the window. Bolan jerked the wheel to the left, banging into the other car, once, again. The driver lost control, jumping the curb and crashing through the guardrail on the side of the bridge. The car plunged sixty feet into Lake Worth, its horn blaring like an air-raid siren.

This was crazy, totally out of control. Bolan wanted to fire again, but civilian traffic and pedestrians were all over the streets, people screaming and running, in the line of fire.

They'd blame him for this one, too.

The limo crossed the bridge, fishtailing a wide right as a hubcap popped loose and flew through the air like a Frisbee. Bolan cut the corner sharper, tighter, the woman's body swaying back and forth.

Behind, cops had managed to pull over several of his pursuers, but not enough. More cops joined the chase on the Palm Beach side of the bridge.

Bolan was closing on Metrano's car as they sped south on Row. Flooring the gas pedal, he caught them as they passed the Breakers Hotel, its exclusive golf course stretching pale green all the way to the white beach of the Atlantic Ocean.

He dropped the Wilkinson and grabbed Big Thunder from the seat. The limo's windows were tinted black. He'd have to pick his shot, figuring Big Tommy to be in the back seat. Just then the front window powered down, the cars inches apart, scenery blurring past.

A riot gun nosed out of the passenger window just as Bolan dropped the hammer on the AutoMag. Empty. He ducked, the shotgun loud in his ears as it tore up the inside of the Lincoln. Still down, he veered into the limo, both vehicles climbing the curb and careering into the golf course.

Metrano's car took off across the wide open fairway, Bolan following. Golf carts darted about in confusion, rats in a maze, as the other cars pursued the first two onto the course, firing away in open country.

Bullets slammed into the Lincoln, and Bolan swerved to make it tougher. He caught a glimpse of the dead woman, his mind racing to fit her into the picture.

The Caddy crested the seventh green, taking out the flag, and jumped the sand trap as it tried to make it back to the street. All Bolan could do was stay close and hope he got a hole in one with the carbine before Metrano made it the three miles to Regents Park and his fortresslike home.

They made County Road, which bisected the course, plunging through the protective rail and onto it, the crew wagon's trunk bouncing up and down with the movements. Bolan followed, laying down a couple of rounds through the open windshield space.

He had started gaining on the limo again, when its driver took a different tack. He swerved off the main road, moving into the wealthy beachfront neighborhoods and their winding streets.

Bolan followed, still hoping for a clean shot, knowing he had to keep moving or die at the hands of those chasing him. It was like some surreal nightmare, everything happening swiftly around him, beyond his control. And in Bolan's line of work, control was everything.

Metrano's sedan turned down Worth Avenue, the most expensive three blocks of real estate in the world, the exclusive shops and restaurants of the superrich stretching out on either side in absurd counterpoint to the filth that was now filtering through it.

Metrano was nearly home. Other cars made the streets, large crowds of weekend pedestrians dodging the speeding vehicles. The cops were all converging, too, flashing lights and sirens turning the atmosphere to a grotesque carnival. Cars took to the wide sidewalks, trash cans flying through the bright afternoon, people diving into storefronts.

A white Cadillac blew a tire and blasted right through the large plate-glass window of Gucci's, the police car behind it swerving into a light post, knocking it into the middle of the street in a cascade of sparks.

Bolan took aim with the carbine, zeroing on the limo's right rear tire, but it swerved around a Mercedes, and he slammed on his brakes instead. This was insane. He dropped the rifle and veered off just as he saw Metrano's car pull up to the gates of his mansion, a squad of men armed with automatics running out to protect their boss.

He sped off quickly, hurrying to lose himself in the maze of residential streets. He'd have to get to safety quickly. The Lincoln was like a red flag, battered and pitted with bullet holes. He jammed the gas pedal and hurried toward the bridge at Southern Boulevard so he could get back to the mainland before the cops could seal it off.

Angrily, he turned to the corpse beside him. "What the hell is going on here?" he asked through clenched teeth.

3

It was twilight before Bolan pulled into the driveway of the ranch-style house he had rented on Riviera Beach. He got out quickly, moving to open the garage. The neighborhood was quiet and residential. Besides the rhythmic slapping of the surf behind the white frame house, the only sound he could hear was the distant echo of rock and roll music. He took note but didn't listen. The gentler arts were something long ago buried within the puzzle box of the Executioner's past, covered fast with the scar tissue of pain and responsibility.

Though he had friends and associates, good people, his fight was, had to be, a lonely one. For when the life you lead keeps you on the ragged territory between survival and death, you find yourself saying goodbye too often. And goodbye in Mack Bolan's world was a permanent thing. He thought of April Rose. She had shared his world, his love and his mission—and when a KGB bullet ended her life in the attack on Stony Man Farm, he was forced to say goodbye, not only to April, but to a good bit of himself.

The fight had continued, for the man known as the Executioner had a mission, but giving of himself emotionally to others was something he guarded himself against. The pain that could hurt him, could kill him, resided within himself. The death of April had almost done it to him. And now he protected himself as best he could, except with Johnny, his brother, who shared some of his lonely vigils.

The door rumbled open and he moved back to the car, driving into the cavern of the garage under the nearly iridescent blue of the rapidly darkening sky. He was tired, emotionally drained from a day of playing hide and seek with the Mob and the Florida police.

He left the headlights on until he got the garage door closed and locked, then he turned them off and moved around to the passenger side and opened the door. The woman's body slumped out into his arms. He probably should have gotten rid of her, but the riddle of her identity was more than he could walk away from. She had been at the church for reasons similar to his own, had died for those reasons, and Bolan had to know why.

He picked her up off the seat. She was surprisingly light, her jump suit still damp from the blood that had stopped flowing now. He moved to the door that led inside. The TV was blaring as he walked into the house. There was a dining table with two folding chairs, and two sleeping bags unrolled on the living room floor. There was no other furniture.

Bolan's brother, Johnny, jumped up from the floor in front of the television when he heard movement in the house. His look of happiness turned to near horror when he saw the grisly bundle Bolan held in his arms.

He ran up, staring into the dead woman's slack face. "Who is it?" he asked.

"You should keep that door locked," Bolan replied. He moved to the table, dropping his burden heavily upon it, fast-food bags and paper cups flying everywhere.

"Sorry, I . . ."

"Lock it now," Bolan growled, and bent to the woman who lay sprawled on the table, her dead eyes staring at the ceiling.

In the living room the television was showing pictures of the savaging of Worth Avenue. It was a national telecast. They were interviewing the chief of the Palm Beach Police.

"It looks like the work of that vigilante, the one they call the Executioner," the officer was saying. "The man he was after, Mr. Metrano, has been under state and federal investigation for quite some time, but so far there's really no evidence to connect him to organized crime."

"The guest list at the wedding would do if you people could read," Bolan said, nodding at the TV.

"What happened out there?" Johnny asked, moving around the other side of the table to look at the woman.

"...All available personnel, including the FBI, are involved in the search for this guy," the chief said. "As of this moment, we are engaged in the largest manhunt in Florida history. We'll have him before long."

"Her accent was French," Bolan said, patting the woman's pockets to see if they contained any clue to her identity. They were, not surprisingly, empty. "Why don't you crank up one of those machines and see if you can find us anything on the word *Sabra*."

"A girl's name?" Johnny asked.

Bolan shook his head, and ripped open the woman's jump suit, tearing it from her body. "An organization, I think. I'm sure she was at the church in a professional capacity."

Johnny moved to the portable computer hardware in the next room and turned on the phone modem that gave him fingers that spread over the whole world.

The woman was wearing only panties under the jump suit, her pale skin encrusted with dried blood. She had no identification of any kind, her only jewelry a fine silver chain on which hung a six-pointed star, a Jewish symbol.

Plan, Bolan thought. Where had he heard that word?

On television, the Cadillac was being winched out of the ocean where it had run off the bridge, with shots interspersed of the bodies being carried away from the wreck, white sheets covering them.

Bolan thought of Devil's Island, of the ingenious way prisoners had of concealing their valuables in small silver cylinders called *plans*. The woman was hiding something. He was sure of it now.

He quickly examined the body, finally moving to her mouth, forcing the already stiffening jaws open. Johnny walked back into the room, puzzlement showing on his face.

"What are you doing, Mack?" he asked.

Bolan looked up, his face hard. "She said something, sounded like *plan*. I think it's a French word," he said. "Maybe she can help us finish what she started. Get me a flashlight and some needle-nose pliers."

Johnny Bolan, only surviving member of Mack Bolan's family, got the tools and left them on the table, returning to his computer silently.

Bolan took the flashlight and played the beam inside the woman's mouth. Her teeth were stained red, forcing him to clean them off with a rag before continuing. When he did, he found a tooth unlike the others, not quite matching in coloration, a little brighter. This had to be it.

Flashlight in one hand, the pliers in the other, Bolan began tugging at the discolored tooth. It came out easily.

"Got it!" Johnny called from the next room, and walked in just in time to see his brother holding a bloody tooth up to the light.

"Tell me," Bolan replied, and laid the tooth on the table.

Johnny sat on a folding chair, facing away from the body. "You know you really tore this city up," he said. "We have to get out of here."

"Soon," Bolan answered, picking up the tooth and wiping the blood off it. "Any civilians hurt?"

Johnny shook his head. "A concussion, a broken arm and a lot of fender benders. Eleven on the other side are dead, though."

Bolan grunted neither satisfaction nor regret, simple acknowledgment. "Sabra," he said again, and found the tooth had a hairline break around its circumference. He turned it against itself and it unscrewed.

"It's a cactus that grows all over Israel," Johnny said.

"Israel," Bolan repeated distractedly, pulling the tooth apart and finding a tiny spool of microfilm within.

"I was able to get into the State Department's computers and checked what they had for Israel." Johnny turned to stare as his brother dumped the microfilm onto the tabletop. "The info is pretty sketchy, just reports from Company people over there, but it seems that Sabra is the name of an Israeli paramilitary unit that operates independently of that government through the private funding of mostly American Jews. They're a strike force that conducts commando raids on PLO targets both inside and outside the country.

The word is that they were the ones responsible for the raid in Tunisia that detroyed the PLO headquarters.''

Bolan stood. "What could they want over here?" He took the pliers and picked up the film by the edge.

Johnny shrugged. "That's all I could find," he said.

Bolan handed him the pliers. "Think you could rig something up so we could get a look at this?"

"Give me five minutes."

While Johnny rummaged through his case Bolan used the time to make sure no trace of them remained in the house. They were going to have to get out quickly, preferably in another vehicle. They'd have to leave all the gear behind, but there was more where that came from.

This was a bad one, and Bolan was worried, not so much for himself, but for his brother. The woman had started it, but in his own haste to follow it up, he had used poor judgment. His dislike of Metrano had canceled out all common sense, and that bothered him. Rationality and a dogged sense of protectiveness toward civilians had been among his chief virtues. Today he had ignored both, and would possibly have to pay for it.

He moved through the house quickly, walking finally to the sliding glass door in back that looked out over the ocean. The water churned wildly, reflecting moonlight on its froth in silver diamonds. He thought he detected movement in the shadows for a second, but he convinced himself it wasn't anything. Still, he made sure that the doors were locked.

Things were ready in the living room. Johnny had hooked up a photographic enlarger and was shooting the image at maximum magnification onto the white wall. Even at that, the picture was small and blurry. Bolan walked right up to the wall and leaned in close to look. It was a letter.

Jamil:
Am sending this by messenger. Hope it finds you well. The deal for the artillery and ordnance is set on this end and is already in motion by conveyance previously discussed. We wish the ten million cash in American money. I am set to arrive in Lebanon on the sixteenth and will see to the money personally. Coming with me will be several associates ready to connect up with your people in drug disbursement. Will advise of carrier by another messenger. This operation marks the first union between our organizations. We guarantee the equipment and I am sending, as a gift, one of my experts in the use of C-4 who will help in planning the destruction of the Zionist landmarks previously discussed. All best from our family to yours.

                                          Metrano

"Jamil?" Johnny said.

"Jamil Arman," Bolan said in a low voice, his fists clenched. "Second in command of the PLO."

"Ten million buys a lot of guns."

"And a lot of lives. The sixteenth is three days from now."

"What are we going to do?"

Bolan turned toward the dining area, taking a quick look at the dead Sabra agent. "We're going to get Metrano," he said, "wherever he is."

4

The man sitting in the black Jaguar watched intensely as a small white Siamese cat crept along the rooftops. It moved along a path it had used for years, leaping from roof to fence to tree and back to roof again, patrolling its territory without ever jumping to the ground. If it saw the Jaguar parked in front of the white frame house that came somewhere toward the middle of its circuit, it didn't let on. More important, it didn't change its routine.

The man in the car smiled when he saw the cat approaching him. He reached under his dark leather bucket seat and pulled out a bundle wrapped in oilcloth. He peeled away the protective covering to reveal a Manurhin MR 73 Long Range with a 9-inch barrel, a formidable .357 Magnum he had brought to the United States in his diplomat's attaché case—personal property of his country's embassy and exempt from customs inspection. The three-inch custom-made silencer was wrapped up with the revolver, and he screwed it in with delicious slowness.

The cat leaped from the roof next to the white frame onto a palm branch, clinging tightly as the branch swayed up and down with its weight. Then the animal raced quickly along the branch and onto another, finally leaping onto the rain gutter of the white frame's roof, and up the eaves to the peak.

The man in the Jag turned on the key so he could operate the power windows. He was Palestinian, and his dark face was framed by a shock of jet-black hair and mustache. Though he had spent many years in the United States, taking advantage of its educational and cultural opportunities, he cherished an intense hatred for Americans. He hated them for what they represented. Though he came from a family made rich by oil, he hated the casual, easygoing life-style that most Americans enjoyed. Life was a war that America hadn't tasted as yet, and the man found in that a profound reason for hating Americans.

He watched the cat climb to the rooftop and walk casually along it, a tiny silhouette moving across a moonlit backdrop. He pushed the button and the window powered up, stopping two-thirds closed.

Whether America knew it or not, World War III had already begun, and the man was one of the advance terrorist troops. It was a war fought not on the usual battlefields, but on the television screens of the world, and the chief weapons in the arsenal were fear and misdirected humanity. Not with a bang would the land of liberty fall—but with a frightened whimper.

The man took out his handkerchief and draped it over the top edge of the half-closed window. Then he laid the barrel of the MR 73 on the handkerchief, leaning close to look down the micrometer rear sight.

He chuckled when he got the animal in the sights. He pulled back the hammer, his finger gently caressing the trigger.

His car phone trilled, but he ignored it and continued tracking the cat. Just before it reached the far end of the roof, he squeezed off a shot, the gun bucking in his hand, its sound a muted hiss, like the closing of elevator doors.

The Magnum dum-dum took off the animal's head cleanly, its spasming body clutching frantically at the roof for several seconds before going slack and rolling down the incline to drop heavily onto the front lawn. The man nodded in satisfaction and reached for the phone. He had just taught some weak American family a lesson in impermanence.

"Yes?"

"Are our people there yet, Abba?"

"No. If they don't come soon, I shall handle this myself."

"Don't be hasty. There's already been enough trouble for one—"

The man hung up the phone, then disconnected the ringer so he couldn't be annoyed by a callback. All Americans were weak, even the Mafia. He had been the only one able to stay with the stranger who pulled the Sabra agent out of the church. The man was probably the one who killed the courier with the letter to Jamil, also. This one had to be taken care of quickly. He was dangerous, not soft like the others.

The black-haired man heard the sound of engines and looked in his rearview mirror to see several cars moving slowly down the street with their headlights off. They coasted up in front of the house, one Cadillac pulling in front of the driveway to block it off.

Abba got out of the Jag, slipped on his silk sport jacket over the black turtleneck sweater he wore. He still held the Magnum in his hand.

Men began filing quietly out of the cars, several of them carrying shotguns. Tommy Metrano's son, Joey, was among them, walking toward Abba as soon as he saw him.

Abba hated Joey Metrano. He was soft and fleshy like all Americans. He cared nothing for the revolutionary struggle and was interested only in what he could acquire for himself.

"Which house?" Joey asked, nearly a whisper.

Abba pointed to the white frame.

"Is he alone?"

Abba shrugged. "What does it matter?"

Joey Metrano's eyes narrowed. He was taller than the Palestinian, probably outweighed him by eighty pounds, but he was scared of him anyway, scared of the meanness that seemed to well up in a never-ending pool behind the man's eyes. Third-generation Mafia, he felt a lot more comfortable in the boardrooms of the Family's legitimate enterprises than he ever would out on a hit.

"We've got to handle this one quietly," Joey said. "There's been enough bad publicity already today to hurt us for years."

Abba smiled wide, his teeth shining brightly in the moonlight. "Bad publicity!" He snorted derisively. Joey tried to hush him. "We simply go up and take the house. Kill the bastards and burn the son of a bitch to the ground."

"No!" Joey rasped. "We're handling this one my way. We'll figure how to take him quietly, then get rid of the body where it won't be found."

Abba's dark eyes flashed. "Is that the way it is to be, then?"

Joey Metrano nodded, caution in his eyes now.

Abba laughed, moving around to the trunk of his car. "There is a truly fearless man in there," he said. "You shall never take him quietly." He opened the trunk and reached into a satchel, coming out with a hand grenade, holding it up in front of Joey's face.

"What's that for?"

Abba held up a finger. "Since you are the leader here, I want to see what your orders will be."

"Give me the grenade," Joey said.

"Yes," Abba said, smiling, and placed the grenade in Joey's palm, pulling the pin as he did.

Metrano stared openmouthed at the live bomb in his hand.

"Whatever you decide to do with it," Abba said, moving away from the man, "I'm going in."

"HOW DO YOU EXPECT to get Metrano in the Mid East if you can't get him here?" Johnny asked, walking up next to Bolan to study the letter projected on the wall.

"I've spent two weeks trying to crack his defenses here," Bolan said. "Besides his goons, the walls around the place are set with glass and floodlit. There are electronic eyes everywhere, along with TV cameras and the manpower to watch them. The lawn around the house is mined and booby-trapped...and I haven't even gotten to the house yet. I'd have a better chance getting into NORAD headquarters. He can't possibly have that kind of protection away from home."

Johnny moved back and shut down the enlarger. "Maybe this one's just too big for us, Mack."

Bolan looked hard at him, understanding his feelings. "Look," he said. "I've got to do this. Ten million dollars' worth of heavy equipment in the hands of terrorists can turn a lot of places into hell on earth." He pointed toward the kitchen. "That's why she died. She gave her life without complaint to stop this, and we don't even know her name. Plus the letter talked about a dope exchange, a new pipeline into this country, a new sewer to kill our kids. Metrano's the enemy. And until the world stops living by jungle law, I have a job to do."

Johnny turned on the overhead light. "I know, Mack. I guess lately I've been worrying too much."

"Why don't you worry about getting us in and out of the country?"

"Sure, I..."

The explosion was like the roar of the wind as the living room wall burst inward in orange fire, part of the ceiling falling as the lights blacked out. The concussion knocked them both back against the far wall, Bolan breaking through Sheetrock to lie half in the dining room.

Head spinning, covered with plaster dust, he pulled out in time to see through the flames an enemy squad charging up the lawn toward them.

5

The warrior moves instinctively. In the time it takes for civilians to react to a crisis, contemplate activity and decide on a course of action, the warrior has already responded in kind. Bolan was up, lifting a still-groggy Johnny to his feet and shoving him around the wall and into the kitchen. Big Thunder was in his plaster-covered hand, spitting death through the flames that were already threatening to turn the house to tinder. A dark figure on the lawn jumped like a puppet, falling in a heap on the ground. One down—but how many more?

They had to move—and quick. If the Executioner never had the odds, at least he usually got to pick his killing ground. This wasn't it. He got around the wall, the house veiled in dark, roiling smoke. Johnny was on his knees, coughing, as their assailants surrounded the house, blasting away, turning the inside of the house into an arcade.

"Get up!" he yelled, coughing. His eyes were burning. "Move toward the garage."

Johnny struggled to his feet, blood oozing from where his head had hit the wall. His hair was matted thickly and he was still disoriented.

There was a loud crash, and more of the ceiling fell in, more fuel for the fire that now raged out of control. As Johnny staggered to the garage door, Bolan looked frantically around for an equalizer. At least the fire was keeping the attackers back. Had they come in without it, he and his brother would probably be dead by now.

He remembered the Ingram MAC-10 stuttergun in the kitchen. He moved through the growing haze to retrieve it, shoving the clip of parabellums to lock into place. A dish towel lay across the sink. He picked it up and ran it under the tap, then tied it around his face like a mask to help with the smoke.

The TV picture tube exploded in the next room. Bolan moved to the living room with the automatic, faced with a wall of fire, and chose his targets through the shooting flames. He raked the area with short bursts, taking some of the attackers to the ground, driving the others back. If they wanted to bring the fight to him, he'd give them all they could handle.

Behind him, Johnny had fumbled open the door leading to the garage, moving into its cavernous darkness. Bolan backed toward it, determined not to let the vermin take him here, now. He reached the door, pulling the towel off his face. The woman still lay on the table and he knew he couldn't abandon her, not like this.

The whole front of the house fell in as he charged back into the dining room and jerked a curtain off the window. Gunfire erupted behind the movement, the glass blowing out the window as Bolan ate carpet.

He came back up, angry, using what was left in the gun on the goons around that side. He threw the empty Ingram to the floor and grabbed the woman, wrapping her in the curtain.

They were pressing close, firing again as he made the garage. Then, for a brief moment, all was dark and calm. Johnny was leaning against the battered Lincoln, breathing deeply.

"You okay?" Bolan asked, moving to the back door, his burden thrown over his shoulder.

Johnny nodded, clearing his throat. "Who is it?"

"Metrano's people," Bolan said, opening the door and throwing the body on the back seat. "There's a Middle Easterner out there, too. We attract a good crowd." They could hear voices yelling, up close. "Thought I'd shaken them all. Let's go!"

"Where?" Johnny said, climbing into the passenger seat.

Bolan jumped in the driver's side and keyed the engine. "Anywhere that's not on fire," he said, and threw the car into reverse, jamming the gas pedal.

The tires squealed loudly and the car broke right through the garage door, wood and glass exploding around them. The second it took to smash into the car blocking the driveway lasted an eternity.

Looking over his shoulder, Bolan saw it coming, but couldn't get his foot to the brake fast enough. They slammed into the car, the impact throwing them backward. The Executioner's arm jammed the horn, as Johnny went half over the back seat.

Bolan pulled his head up in time to see ten men with guns turn toward him and take aim. He banged the gear shift with an open hand, the transmission locking on the Drive position, and hit the gas. The forward momentum hurled Johnny back onto the seat.

In front of them a man stood splay-legged, his .38 raised. They hit him head-on, the lethal impact throwing him onto the hood. Then the garage blurred past and they crashed through the other side. The gunner slithered off the hood and onto the lawn. Bolan felt a brief jolt as the Lincoln's radials rolled over the body.

The terrain dropped steeply in the back of the house and the Lincoln raced down a slope, nearly capsizing before reaching the level beach.

They spun off through the loose sand, wide arcing sprays spewing up from the back wheels. Metrano's soldiers were giving chase on foot, still dangerous, even from a distance.

Bolan drove toward the hard-packed sand closer to the water. The ocean looked inviting, soothing. He resisted an impulse to drive into the water, and turned hard, speeding along the waterline, the sound of gunfire becoming more distant by the second.

TOMASSO METRANO STOOD looking down at the mangled body of his son. The father held a handkerchief up to his nose to ward off the dissipating smoke, and he knew that no one could tell precisely what caused the moisture-filled eyes. Except, of course, Big Tommy himself. Joey had never been all that he had hoped, but he had been a good boy and had always tried to please his father. This was no way for a Metrano to die, ground up like hamburger under the wheels of a car. It was his own fault, really. He should never have sent the boy to do a man's job.

The Executioner's house was nothing but smoking ruins, the fire department mopping up the remnants, hosing water on any embers. Police and ambulances filled the streets, taking away more of Metrano's people. This was going to cost a bundle to keep quiet. He was liable to have to juice them all the way up to Tallahassee.

He turned from Joey's body and the huge hole in the back of the garage, and looked toward the sea. Abba, his PLO contact, was staring in the direction the bastard had taken.

Metrano moved his six-foot-five, three-hundred-pound frame to stand beside the man. "What happened here?" he asked softly.

Abba just touched him with his dark eyes, then looked back toward the ocean. "Your son wanted to go in," he said. "I told him I had a better plan. But he would not listen." He pointed down the beach. "We have to find that son of a whore. I have seen his kind before. He is crazy. He will do anything."

"What happened to my boy?"

Abba shrugged matter-of-factly. "They ran him over like pita bread. Maybe we should postpone the exchange until we kill this bastard?"

"No," Metrano said quickly. The truth was he couldn't afford to postpone the trip. The Executioner had cost him millions in cash he desperately needed to keep his organization fluid.

"Did he die like a man?" he asked.

The Palestinian's eyes held a question. He turned and looked back at the body. Two men were loading it onto a stretcher, covering the remains of Joey Metrano with a white sheet. "He died," Abba said. "Everything dies. Why? Do you give out medals for bravery like the army?" He laughed at his own joke.

"I want him," Metrano said, a whisper. "I don't care what you have to do to get him, but I want him. He's gonna die slow, you understand?"

Abba nodded, smiling.

Big Tommy pulled a cigar out of his suit coat pocket and stuck it into his mouth. "And when it comes time to kill him..." He pulled his cigar out and pointed it at his chest. "I'm gonna be the one to do it."

Abba laughed gently, his eyes dancing. Maybe America wasn't such a bad place after all.

Metrano turned and walked off, through the hole in the garage and back out front, watching as they loaded Joey's body into the ambulance. Police were waiting to talk to him, but for what he paid a year in pad money, he felt they could wait a month for him.

Joey had never been very good at Family business, but his mother had loved him and telling her was going to be a pain in the ass. Of his three sons, Joey had been the worst. Because he was the youngest, his mother had babied him. He had sent the dumb shit out to try and make a man out of him, but it didn't work out.

Tomasso Metrano turned his back to the warm night air and lit the cigar. He knew one thing, the bastard who was dogging him had taken his last shot. The Executioner had just gone from being a nuisance to a priority.

MACK BOLAN GENTLY LOWERED the unidentified body into the grave they had dug on the beach. They were isolated, far from Metrano's people, from any houses or roadways, with only the steady pounding of the waves for company.

They had pulled off a door panel and the glove compartment lid to help with the digging. It had taken them a long time with the makeshift tools, and those Bolan placed carefully in the grave with the woman. He straightened, then bent back down and as an afterthought removed the woman's Star of David necklace and put it in his pocket.

Johnny had been sitting on the fender of the ravaged car, watching the field burial. The cut on his head had been cleaned and bandaged, thanks to the medical kit that Bolan had kept in the Lincoln's trunk. Now Johnny jumped off the car and moved to the grave, helping his brother shovel armloads of sand back into the six-foot-deep hole.

"You said her accent was French," Johnny said. "How does that fit in with Israeli intelligence?"

"Israel is considered a homeland to all Jews," Bolan replied, using his hands to fill the hole. "Wherever they're from, they can have automatic citizenship in Israel."

They finished up, smoothing out the area.

"You're determined to go over there, aren't you?"

Bolan nodded, his face a mask. "I've got to. You've got misgivings?"

"Plenty."

Bolan pointed to his gut. "I go with what's in here," he said. "I can't know about this and not do anything."

"Yeah, I know."

They stood, dusting off their pants. Bolan turned and looked at the battered car. They couldn't use it anymore. He decided to drive it farther down the beach and abandon it. Later he'd send cash to the rental company to pay for the thing. "We're going to have to go underground while I raise some cash," he said.

"Maybe Miami," Johnny said. "Somewhere in the barrio."

Bolan nodded. "It suits." He looked down at the ground, surprised that he couldn't immediately place the grave site they had just dug. "Guess we're done here."

"Yeah" was all the younger Bolan said.

They climbed back into the car. Bolan had to try three times before he got it started. He put it in gear and they rattled on down the beach.

"You know," Bolan said loudly over the engine noise, "you mustn't feel obligated to involve yourself with the overseas mission. In fact, I'd prefer if you stayed out of it. I can handle it myself."

Johnny laughed, then grimaced with the pain in his head. "Somebody's got to keep you out of trouble," he replied.

"Well, you've done a hell of a job so far," Bolan said.

6

Bolan moved up the long flight of narrow wooden stairs, the smell of urine strong in the confined space. It was dark in there even in the middle of the day, the walls on either side filthy and scrawled with spray-painted graffiti proclaiming the names of the neighborhood Cuban street gangs that claimed the place as part of their turf.

The Executioner's false Vandyke beard was itchy where the spirit gum held it in place. A briefcase dangled from his left hand. He wore a brown three-piece suit, the silenced Beretta 93-R nestled snugly under his left arm. He was going to the Bank of Metrano to make a withdrawal.

A Cuban whore stood two-thirds of the way up the stairs, all legs under her black leather microskirt. She smacked gum loudly while filing her long black nails that looked like talons with an emery board. At Bolan's approach, she braced herself against the wall and raised a black-stockinged leg to the other side, blocking his advance.

"Hey, good looking," she said, blowing a bubble. "Need your plumbing overhauled?"

"Some other time, maybe," he said, moving her leg and walking past.

"I've got your time right here," she called up to him, and went back to work on the claws.

Bolan crested the stairs and walked down a narrow hallway, stopping in front of a door with Ecstasy Inc. written on the dirty glass. He went in.

A pudgy, pink-looking man sat behind a desk, sleeves of his white shirt rolled up to the elbows. A nameplate, identifying him as Larry Price, manager, sat on the desk. There was a tattered sofa across from the desk, and several doors led out of the office and into other rooms. In the back he could hear women moaning in mock rapture.

The man snorted, wiping his nose with the back of his hand. "How do?" he said in a gravel voice, and stood.

"I'm looking for a little...relaxation," the Executioner said, smiling.

"Well, you've come to the right place, brother," Larry replied, stepping out to shake hands. "We got relaxation in all shapes and sizes."

Bolan took the man's hand, twisting it violently behind his back. "Okay, Larry," Bolan said quietly, into the man's ear. "We're going to get into the safe and see what there is to see. Where is it?"

"On the wall," the guy returned. "Please don't hurt me."

"You'll only get what you got coming."

Larry moved toward a framed picture on the wall. Bolan unholstered the 93-R and let him get a look at it.

The manager dialed the combination. "I just work here," he said. "I don't have nothin' to do with nothin'."

"That's not what the girl I visited in intensive care said last night," Bolan said, jamming the Beretta's snout into the base of the guy's skull. "At least as much as she could talk around the wires holding her jaw together."

"Hey, you got to make these bitches respect you, right?"

"Right," said Bolan, jerking the arm upward.

The man yelped in pain, and Bolan released him after he felt his captive got the message. He massaged his shoulder for a moment, then reached out, fumbling with the dial on the wall safe.

The safe swung open, and for just an instant Larry let his eyes flick toward one of the other doors. Bolan caught the motion, the hairs prickling on the back of his neck.

He swung around, the 93-R tracking, just as the door flew open, two men with 12-gauge pump shotguns jumping through.

Bolan fired, drilling one through the neck before he even took aim. The gun flew from the hood's hands, his momentum carrying him across the room to crash through the front door, glass breaking loudly. Bolan heard the whore on the stairs screaming.

The other hood fired as Bolan dived to the floor and rolled, wood splintering under the heavy gauge right beside him. He returned fire as the button pumped, his right thigh exploding, knocking him back against the wall. The hood fired again, blowing a large gash in the front wall. Bolan came up high this time, his shot shearing away the man's lower jaw.

The mobster's eyes widened as he slid to the floor, looking like some hideous mutant. He fell to his side, blood running freely from the gaping hole in his head to pool on the dirty floor.

Bolan spun to the pudgy manager in time to see him pulling a .45 automatic out of the safe. He pounced on the man, slamming his hand in the heavy safe door to make him drop the gun. The manager rolled away, nursing his shattered wrist.

"What were they doing here?" the Executioner demanded.

"I don't know," Larry sobbed, tears rolling down his cheeks. "They showed up this morning, said they were waiting on somebody."

A setup. Big Tommy was going all out. Bolan wondered if he should be flattered.

Another inner door burst open, men and women in various stages of undress running through the office and outside, past the corpse in the hall. Bolan could hear their footsteps pounding down the stairway.

Bolan stared hard at the front-office guy. "You got anything else for me?"

"No," the man whined. "That's it. They wouldn't tell me anything. Please believe me."

"I do believe you," Bolan said. "Now turn around."

"Please don't shoot me in the back, mister."

"Don't worry, I haven't got ammo to waste," the Executioner said, and brought the butt of the 93-R down behind the man's ear. He dropped like a stone.

Bolan reholstered the weapon and brought the briefcase over to the safe. The bills were banded and stacked in piles of ten. Bolan quickly loaded it all into the valise, then took out the large plastic bag full of white powder he found in there with the cash.

He opened the bag. Licking his index finger, he dipped it into the contents, smearing a small amount on his gums, feeling the numbing sensation. Cocaine, nearly pure.

He used his arm to sweep everything off the desk, then poured the coke all over its top. He smoothed it out, then used a finger to write, TOMASSO ME-TRANO, in the powder.

Then he called the police and told them about the shooting. When he hurried back down the stairs, the hooker was long gone.

THE LUNCH CROWD in the Rice Bowl was large and noisy. The Chinese and Cubans from the neighborhood were all regulars, laughing and yelling to one another from table to table.

Bolan parked the beat-up Volkswagen out front and walked through the open door, waving to May, the teenage daughter of the owner, Mr. Wong, as she punched the cash register.

The kitchen was at the very back of the place, behind a large window cut into a dividing wall for the placing and receiving of orders. A swinging door was set beside the window, and Bolan moved familiarly through it.

The kitchen was a confusion of chopping blocks, woks, rice cookers, cleavers, Chinese chatter and wonderful smells as the three cooks hustled through lunch rush. Instantly, memories of R and R in Southeast Asia stirred in Bolan's brain.

Johnny was leaning against a white tile wall near the pay phone, its receiver cradled on his shoulder as he wrote on a notepad. When he caught sight of his brother, he waved, then got quickly off the phone.

Bolan raised an eyebrow and motioned his brother back toward the room attached to the kitchen, which they had rented the night before from an ad in the Miami *Herald*.

"How'd it go?" Johnny asked, as he followed Bolan into the small room.

"They've been waiting for me all over town," Bolan replied, closing the door. "But we came out all right."

The room was just barely that. Two small beds and a night table between them.

Bolan put the briefcase on the bed and opened it. Johnny whistled when he saw the stacks of bills tumbling out. "How much?"

"Haven't counted," the Executioner said, and closed the case. "But it'll do. How's it going on this end?"

Johnny frowned, opening the notepad to the first page. "I've been using Kurtzman's computers long distance," he said. "It's taken all morning, but I'm not sure what I came away with."

"Let me hear it."

"I've checked all the commercial airlines, and there's no record of Metrano leaving the country on any of them. He could be using forged papers, but I saw no groups of travelers that looked suspicious on the flight plans."

"How about boats?" Bolan asked, as he tugged at the itchy beard to get it off.

"Nothing that could have Metrano on it," he said, flipping a page. "And I've been checking on the guns. Nothing obvious has gone out, although I've got something that strikes me as suspicious. The *Latva*, a freighter with Greek registry, sailed from Miami several days ago en route to Haifa, the chief Israeli port. Its manifest lists it as carrying several tons of wheat."

"So?" Bolan had the beard off and was rubbing his chin.

"I've been doing some checking on Israel," Johnny replied. "It's a country desperately striving for self-sufficiency, and it has to import most of its goods, which really screws up the economy. The end result is that they work hard to produce as much in country as possible. One of the things they grow..."

"Wheat!" Bolan said.

"Right. They not only grow enough for their own needs, but even manage to export a bit. So, about the last thing in the world they'd import is something they have enough of."

"That's our ship," Bolan said, taking off the suit coat and hanging it in the small, freestanding closet in the corner. "When does it dock?"

"Day after tomorrow."

"We've got to get out of here. Have you found us a pilot?"

"Grimaldi can handle it," Johnny said, and closed the notebook. "But there's something else."

Bolan could see that Johnny was troubled. He sat on the bed opposite, loosening his tie. "What's wrong?"

"This whole deal," Johnny said. "I'm afraid it's our fault."

"How?"

"I've been correlating police reports, Mack." Johnny stared down at the floor. "Over the past several months, all the hits you've made on Metrano's places across the country have been followed up by break-ins at armories and factories near the same locations. I think this is where Big Tommy's gotten the guns to deal with the PLO."

Bolan felt the wind go out of him. "You think he's using this to make up for all the blood we've been taking out of him."

Johnny nodded, finally meeting Bolan's eyes. "Because of us, he needs the money. Because of us, he's selling heavy artillery to terrorists."

Mack Bolan looked at his brother.

"Maybe," he said. "But somehow I don't think so. You don't know these savages like I do. The man's pure evil."

7

From its Mediterranean harbor, Acco, Israel, looked exactly like what it was—a citadel. Even now, in the dark of night, its strength and history could be felt. During the Crusades, it had been the chief European stronghold in the wars to take Jerusalem from the Muslims. Richard the Lionhearted had fought Saladin here. Centuries later, Napoleon Bonaparte threw himself against the same stone walls in an unsuccessful attempt to drive the vicious Turks from Syria.

Mack Bolan found those walls no more inviting.

He and Johnny paddled to shore, the high walls stretching all around them. The small city was protected on three sides by water. Ancient Turkish cannons still pointed out to sea from the crenels, but their glory was long faded, their firepower a memory.

The Bolans had left the United States the day before, Jack Grimaldi getting them secretly to Cyprus. From there they had taken a fishing boat to within the three-mile limit, using the rubber raft for the rest of the trip. They carried neither passports nor identification. If they were caught, even by the people they were trying to help, they would be dealt with as ene-

mies. For Israel was a country with a great many enemies and, like Mack Bolan, it felt the necessity of
dealing with them quickly and with finality.

The shore was rocky and uninviting. They paddled
toward a wide flat rock, the current washing them violently up against it. They climbed out quickly, drag-
ging their heavy duffels full of ordnance onto the
shore at the base of the walls. Bolan took a K-bar
knife from the duffel and hacked a hole through the
raft, watched it sink into the dark, swirling waters.
They were in. They'd worry about getting out when
the time came.

Johnny hoisted his duffel over his back with some
effort and stared straight up the length of the high
walls. He shook his head in dismay.

"Follow me," Bolan said, picking up his own bag.

He walked off, moving next to the wall, studying its
contours.

The Executioner was not the first man to land ille-
gally on these beaches. When the British controlled
Israel and strictly curtailed Jewish immigration,
thousands of Jews found their way into the homeland
the same way Bolan did—by night, on the shores between Acco and Haifa.

"Here," Bolan said, pointing to an opening in the
wall.

Johnny walked up beside him to see a small tunnel,
barricaded by an iron grating, in the solid stone.

"The Crusaders built several of these in the twelfth
century," Bolan said. "In case they got trapped in the

city, these were escape passages to the sea. They've been left open for the tourist trade. This will get us into the heart of the city.''

He got a small crowbar out of his pack, and they spent the next quarter of an hour prying the bars open enough for them to slip through.

They entered the tunnel, so small they had to crouch-walk. The pounding of the sea echoed all through the hewed-stone cavern; Bolan's flashlight beam sent rats scurrying for safety.

''Shouldn't we have landed closer to Haifa?'' Johnny asked.

''This is a tourist spot,'' Bolan replied, ''but not at night. The city itself is basically an Arab slum and the locals don't get along with the Israelis very well. We'll be safe here for tonight. Haifa's close enough that we can get there in the morning.''

The tunnel exited into a huge stone room eight hundred years old. Mammoth pillars ran through the large space, the ceilings fifty feet overhead. Their footsteps rang hollowly as they walked through an ancient warriors' banquet hall.

They climbed many stairs, finally finding moon-light again in a medieval courtyard, an open doorway leading into the city.

It was late, most of the inhabitants long asleep. But Bolan wasn't interested in them anyway. It was the people of the night he wanted, the people who did things that cannot be done in the light of day.

They walked the cobbled streets, past the mixture of Crusader, Turk and modern slum buildings. Down a narrow, foul-smelling alley they found what they were looking for. A tavern, reeking of cheap wine and urine, threw dirty light into the night.

They walked in, the eight or ten patrons, all male, glaring at them. The man behind the bar hurried to intercept them before they got too far inside. He was short and swarthy, his three-day growth of beard salted with gray to match the streaks in his greasy black hair.

"This place for Arab," he said in a thick accent. "You go to place for Americans."

"I think this'll do," Bolan said, returning the bartender's gaze. "We want a room for the night, no questions asked."

Several of the patrons had moved away from the rough wooden tables to surround the pair. A lean young man in a torn undershirt and stained khaki pants prodded Bolan's duffel.

"What you got in bag, rich American?" he said softly, "Maybe a present for me?"

Bolan smiled widely, then came around hard with an elbow to the youth's gut, doubling him over. Turning, the Executioner grabbed him by his hair and pulled, running his head right into the bar. The man collapsed onto the dirty floor.

The others tensed, the room suddenly silent. Mack Bolan smiled easily.

"Now," he said, and pulled a hundred-dollar bill out of his pocket, showing it around the room. "Can't we all be friends?"

The barman grabbed the bill, pocketing it immediately. "I got a good room upstairs, just for you."

Bolan pulled out another bill, holding it up. "This is for as much as anyone wants to drink tonight." The guy on the floor was beginning to stir. "Buy him a whole bottle," Bolan said.

TOMASSO METRANO WAS HAVING a difficult time hearing on the telephone over the screaming in the next room. "What did you say?" he yelled, hand over his other ear as he strained to make contact through static with the voice on the American end.

It was no use. "Just a minute!" he yelled again, and turned to his son, Guido. "Would you do somethin' to shut off that racket. I can't hear myself think."

"Sure, Pop," Guido said, and moved across the gaudy, plush room to the attached interrogation chamber.

They were in Jamil Arman's underground headquarters, sequestered in the foothills that separated Israel from Lebanon. Arman hadn't as yet arrived, but all of Metrano's people were there, including his two remaining sons, Guido and Tony.

American weapons were piled everywhere, including mortars and hand-carried SAMs. On the dining table in the long room, Big Tommy's chemist was testing the potency of a five-kilo bag of processed heroin.

Guido Metrano was not too bright, but he loved his work, especially the dirty stuff. He smiled when he walked into the interrogation room. His brother, Tony, along with Abba, were taking turns skinning the Israeli Mossad agent they had caught earlier that day. Both men were stripped to the waist so as not to mess up their shirts with blood. The agent hung from the ceiling by his arms, leaving him totally vulnerable.

"That's not the way," Abba was saying to Tony Metrano. "Take a wider strip and do not cut down so deep. He will die too soon. Watch."

He moved to the dying man's chest, already a mass of torn flesh and open wounds. "You must go in sideways," Abba said, choosing a section along the operative's rib cage, under his left arm. He traced the blade's point along the skin, angling the knife nearly parallel to the body. Pain gurgled up through the Israeli's clenched teeth.

"Then you jerk quickly downward, like this...."

Abba pulled hard, his thumb holding flesh on the flat of the blade. The man screamed savagely as a wide, six-inch strip of dermis tore from his convulsing body.

"Wow," Tony said. "You got a real way with that thing."

"Practice," Abba said. "Practice."

"Pop wants you guys to cool it," Guido said. "He's trying to talk overseas."

"Shut the door," Abba said. "The room is sound-proof."

"Great," Guido said, closing the door. "Can I take a crack at that, too?"

THE SCREAMING STOPPED ABRUPTLY and Big Tommy relaxed immediately, returning to his usual good humor. That torture stuff was for the young ones. It only made him nervous to listen to it, like drinking too many cups of coffee.

"Okay," he said into the receiver. "What's the story?"

The voice was distant-sounding, barely audible. "We tracked him as far as Miami International, then lost him. I think he took a plane."

"How could he . . . ? The cops have got to be looking for him."

"Same way you did, Mr. Metrano. He ripped us off pretty good in Miami, came away with enough juice to buy nearly anything."

"You don't think he's comin' here, do you?"

"I don't know. He's like a bulldog once he latches on to something. You gotta kill him to get him off."

"We'll keep our eyes open," Metrano said. "If being dead's what the son of a bitch wants, we'll fix him up here same as home. They got a whole army to deal with him here. Okay, Vinnie. I'll worry about it on this end."

"So long, Mr. Metrano."

Tommy Metrano hung up, confident that he'd finally be able to get the bulldog's teeth out of his rump.

8

If Israel could be described as a body, Jerusalem would be its heart, Tel Aviv its raucous soul and Haifa its pumping lifeblood. Most of the commerce coming into or going out of the country comes through the port of Haifa—a beautiful, sprawling city that literally climbs the side of Mount Carmel right into the bright haze that usually covers it.

Mack Bolan and his brother had taken a *sherut*, a seven-passenger bus, from Acco to Haifa, a short coastal run, and now stood on one of Haifa's many wharves, watching the *Latva* being loaded in record time. Both men wore light jackets, as large as they could get away with in the perpetually warm climate. Both were heavily armed beneath.

The *Latva* was a large freighter. It rode anchor at the end of the dock that extended from the covered wharf, large crates being unloaded by crane into the backs of waiting trucks.

"I can't believe they'd do that right here," Johnny said.

"Makes perfect sense," Bolan countered. "The population here is nearly half Arab, most of them honest and law-abiding. But terrorists are a part of the mix, and it's pretty hard to tell the difference. Probably a lot of that shipment is legitimate, with the contraband well hidden. If they can bring it in under the authorities' noses, it can be distributed across the rest of the country very quickly. If they had to try and sneak it over the border a piece at a time, it would be a lot harder."

"Then these trucks we're watching drive away could be filled with hardware...."

"Or maybe just cabbages," Bolan finished.

Another truck rumbled down the dock toward them, turning onto the wharf, then disappearing into the city. They couldn't just stand there and watch millions of dollars' worth of death leak into the lives of innocent people.

"What do we do?" Johnny asked.

Bolan looked at his watch. It was 10:00 a.m. "First we've got to stop them from loading any more trucks. Then find the heavy stuff."

"What about the authorities?" Johnny asked. "What if we just called them anonymously and told them about the contraband? They could probably handle it better than us anyway."

"Uh-uh," Bolan said. "Even if they *did* take an anonymous call seriously, there'd be too much red tape before a massive search of an already cleared vessel could be mounted. Besides, the Port Authority would be mad as hell and wouldn't admit they could be wrong if anything was found. Meantime, the unloading continues unchecked because they won't call a quarantine without a more probable cause than an anonymous phone call. Of course, we could go to them in person, but then we'd be doing all our explaining from a jail cell.''

"This is crazy."

"It's the way of the world, Johnny," Bolan said. "That's why we're here—to cut through the nonsense."

"When?"

"Right now."

Bolan began walking casually toward the freighter, where a large dockside crane was slowly swinging toward the ship, directed by a sailor on board.

Johnny hurried to catch up, surprised when his brother moved to the side of the dock and stopped at a small snack bar that served wharf employees. The dock was crowded with people, a bad situation if trouble erupted.

The Executioner moved up to the serving window, his eyes expertly scanning the moving crowds for signs of hostiles. "Good morning," he said to the man who came to take his order.

"Shalom," the man replied tiredly.

"Do you speak English?"

Johnny walked up beside Bolan.

"Sure," the man replied, brightening. "I'm from New York. Moved over here after the Six Day War." He reached out and shook hands. "Good to see somebody from the States."

"How about an orange juice," Bolan said, "and a little information."

Israel was famous for its oranges, and orange juice was sold everywhere. "One shekel and a half," the man said, cutting an orange, and putting it on the squeezer. "Info's free to another American."

Bolan put the money up on the counter. "That ship out there . . . what's the story?"

The man shrugged, putting the other half of the orange on the squeezer. "Came in the middle of the night, I guess. At least it was here when I showed up this morning. They've been unloading since first light."

Bolan winced. Three to four hours of unloading sounded like a two-day hangover. "Ever seen that one before?"

The man shook his head. "It's new to me," he said. "Kinda strange how the trucks have been lined up for it, too. Usually they just pile stuff on the dock and it sits. Not this time, though."

"Thanks," Bolan said, and took the juice without even tasting it.

Johnny followed him as he walked toward the ship. "What do you want me to do?" he asked.

"Hang back," Bolan replied. "Cover me if I need it."

He moved off, Johnny slowing his pace to a casual stroll. Bolan could feel the MAC-10 pressed under his left arm.

The crane had creaked into position above the forward cargo hold, and was just lowering its cable when he reached it. The operator was intently watching the man on deck for instructions, and Bolan slipped easily behind the machine and began using a small screwdriver on the bolts that held the square metal housing for the electrical housing.

He removed three bolts, the cover hinging on the fourth to swing open. A maze of large transformers and wiring filled the space.

A gangway stretched from the dock to the deck thirty feet above. Once he put the crane out of commission, he'd have to get up there quickly.

He looked around easily, took a sip of the juice just to try it, then tossed the whole cupful into the exposed wiring.

The unit began arcing loudly, sparks sizzling while bright white smoke poured out of the housing. The whole crane howled as if it were crying, then froze up with a terrible grinding sound, a transformer humming loudly, then blowing. Smoke billowed out of the machine, as people from all over the dock hurried up to see what the problem was.

Bolan raced for the gangway in the confusion, but something tangled up in his legs, sending him sprawling on the dock. He rolled, recovering, but came up into a crouch to face the muzzles of three Uzi submachine guns, one wielded by a woman.

"Amad!" the woman ordered, motioning with her gun.

Bolan smiled, playing dumb. *"Shalom, shalom,"* he said, tensing for a barrel roll. He could take two down at once, counting on Johnny for the third. A second before the lurch, something flashed around the woman's neck and he froze in place.

"Johnny, no!" he shouted, and guns swung around to Johnny Bolan, who stood not five feet distant with his hands away from his body.

The warriors were taken.

Bolan straightened slowly, his hands behind his head. Several more men joined the band, forming a loose circle around them. The Executioner found himself staring into the cold eyes of people to whom death was no stranger.

He said one word to them. *"Sabra."*

TOMMY METRANO STOOD amid the bombed-out ruins of the old PLO base three miles from the Israeli border. It was nothing but a junkyard of charred lumber and stone now, and the carcasses of military vehicles, gutted by fire and stripped by vandals.

The base stood at the top of a hill, within mortar range of the border, and rocket range of any target within Israel. Terrorist raids had been carried out from there on a regular basis until the Israelis cleared it out on their march to Beirut in '82.

Big Tommy was agitated. Not only had he not been able to find decent food, but jet lag and the difference in time zones had kept him from his usual restful sleep. Now he was having to wait on Arman in this godforsaken place, when all he wanted was his ten mil and Bolan's ass.

His entourage of eight was with him, including Abba, who seemed to be the only one around who really knew what was going on. The three black Mercedes sedans they had arrived in were idling a short distance away.

"So where is he?" he asked Abba. "We been here thirty minutes already. I ain't used to bein' kept waitin'."

"He will arrive very soon," Abba said, his dark eyes laughing the way they always did when he talked with the Americans. Big Tommy was willing to give a guy the benefit of the doubt, but he was beginning to suspect that the man was going to have to be taught a little respect before long.

"Well, I'm gettin' sick of waitin'," Metrano said, wiping sweat from his forehead on a handkerchief. "I've kept my end of the bargain. I expect your boss to do the same."

"Jamil Arman is an honorable man," Abba said, voice tight. "He is a soldier fighting an honorable cause. Money is not important to us like it is to you. You shall have all you want."

Metrano moved up closer to him, towering over him. "Listen to me, little man. At least with a few bucks you can look out for yourself, your family. That makes sense. All you people want to do is kill and blow things up. I got a look at Beirut when I was coming into the airport. You dumb shits blow your *own* stuff up."

"Our cause is just," Abba said, angry. "What can you know of our revolutionary struggle?"

Big Tommy spit on the ground. "I know that it makes a lot of fools march off to get their asses blown off, while somebody else sits behind making speeches and getting rich." He started laughing then, Abba turning away.

"Hey, Mr. Metrano!" Arnie called from the cars. "I got Mario on the phone in here."

"There." Abba pointed to a dust cloud in the distance. "He comes."

Metrano strained his eyes to get a good look. A car was racing along a dirt road a mile and a half away, the same road they had taken up to the outpost. He turned back to Arnie and waved his arm. "What's he want?" he called.

"Trouble at the boat, some sort of commotion. People with guns."

"How much we got off already?"

"Two-thirds."

Metrano took a cigar out of this pocket, thinking as he pulled the cellophane wrapper off the thing. He stuck it in his mouth. "Tell them to stick with it, but if it looks like they're in trouble, have them scuttle the load. Blow it up."

"Okay."

Metrano turned and watched the car, another Mercedes, wind its way up the hillside. Maybe now they could get this taken care of and get on with things.

A minute later, the dust cloud pulled into camp, two men in olive-drab uniforms jumping out of the car. They each carried a Valmet Bullpup on full auto with Kalashnikov AK action. They swung the carbines around in a full circle, only letting Arman out of the back seat when they were sure it was safe.

The man got out. He wore an American business suit, with a red-and-white-checked *ghutra* on his head. The double banded *aghal*, a camel rein, was wrapped around it. He was massively overweight, his eyes nearly lost in the large folds of skin that wagged on his face. He wore black-rimmed glasses and a week's growth of beard.

He moved right for Big Tommy, hand extended. "It is my great honor and pleasure to meet you at last, Mr. Metrano." He was soft-spoken, his English impeccable, his voice low and melodious.

"Likewise," Metrano said, shaking hands. "Did you bring the money with you?"

Arman smiled, pouting out his large lower lip. "A man who gets right to the heart of the matter," he said. "I appreciate that in an associate."

"Yeah. Well, the boat's in and the trucks are on the road," Metrano said, wiping his forehead again. "Where I come from you get your business done in a hurry and get off into the shade, y'know?"

"I do indeed understand," Arman returned. "But unfortunately, I do not have the money with me here."

Big Tommy looked around at his men. They were easing toward cover, preparing to handle things. "Where is it?"

"Do not worry, my friend." Arman gestured around the compound with an expansive arm. "This, as you can see, is hardly the safest spot for conducting...delicate business."

"Why are we here then?"

"We are here to—how do you Americans say it?—get on the same wavelength."

Metrano didn't like this guy at all. He talked all the time, but never said anything. "Well, I don't know nothin' about any of that. I just figured to take the cash and haul ass."

Arman moved to put an arm around Big Tommy's shoulder, directing him to look out over the surrounding hills. "Out there," he said, "is the Jewish entity."

"Huh?"

"You call it Israel."

"Oh."

"That land belongs to me and my people, the land of Ibrahim, of Muhammad...the land of Allah." Arman made a fist, shaking it at the sky. "But the cursed Israelis have stripped it from us and forced us to live as nomads. With their ancient ways and heathen minds, they refuse to accept our faith and so must suffer the torments of the Koran."

He walked around in a circle, his hands in the air. "The ground they call their own will soak through with their blood, and the blood of their women, and the blood of their cursed children. We will take back what is rightfully ours and drive their memory from the earth itself." He pointed to Metrano. "And you will help provide the means to do it. Tonight, we move. Tomorrow, we dine in Palestine. And then, when we have tasted Israeli blood together, you will have your money."

"I'll be honest with you," Metrano said. "I ain't too much on politics. You know, outside of what a little juice money will do for you."

Arman walked Big Tommy to the other side of the hill, pointing into Lebanon. "My men await. Ready to die for Allah, for a Palestinian homeland."

He took out a handkerchief, waving it over his head. From behind every bush, every stand of rocks as far as they could see, men stood, dressed in black. There must have been a thousand of them.

"Human bombs," Abba said. "Suicide troops. All are willing to die to fulfill the will of Allah."

"Suicide?" Big Tommy said.

"What do you think of our revolutionary struggle now?" Abba asked, triumphant.

"Son of a bitch" was all Big Tommy could think of to say.

9

Mack and Johnny Bolan stood behind the wharf snack stand, disarmed as much as was humanly possible—for as long as the Executioner's body and mind were intact, he was still the most dangerous weapon in existence. He had played his cards this way intentionally, and now was the time to see if his gamble would turn away the barrels of the submachine guns trained unwaveringly on him and Johnny.

"You don't have much time," he said.

Seven people held him at bay, two of them women, both wearing Stars of David the way the dead agent had. In Israel, military service was compulsory for everyone, male and female, and these women had the thin, taut air of combat veterans. If they were anything like the woman he'd fought beside in Palm Beach, they'd be hell on wheels.

A back door led into the snack stand. The man he had gotten information from earlier came out the door, taking off his white apron. His sleepy look had hardened to granite.

He fixed Bolan with steel-gray eyes. "You've got five minutes to make us love you before we cut your throats and throw you in the ocean," he said.

Bolan held those eyes and spoke volumes in a look, one warrior to another. "New York cop," he said. "SWAT, most likely, and probably Special Forces before that."

The hint of a smile flashed across the man's face. "Nat Barlow," he replied. "And I make you out to be a crazy man."

"Can I reach into my pocket?" Bolan asked.

"Slowly," Barlow said. "Very slowly."

Bolan reached into his pocket and fished out the six-pointed star he had taken from the dead woman, plus the tooth containing the microfilm. He laid them in Barlow's open hand.

The man held up the tooth. "Where did you get this?" he asked.

"I pried it out of a dead woman's mouth."

One of the women, tall with kinky black hair, gasped loudly. "Sara..."

"Quiet," Barlow said to the woman, then to Bolan, "How did she die?"

"With a gun in her hand," Bolan replied, "killing vermin."

"How do you know?"

"I was with her. You're wasting time."

Barlow's expression didn't change. "Why are you here?"

"To stop that ship from unloading millions of dollars' worth of terrorist death into your country. A Mafia family is supplying weapons and ordnance to the PLO."

"Why would an American care about what happens to Israel?"

"You're an American," Bolan said. "You care."

Barlow looked at his watch. "The five minutes is up...you've made it." He nodded to the others, and they brought down their guns and began talking all at once, looking at the effects of their dead sister.

"Tell me about the boat," Barlow said, and Bolan quickly recounted the events of the past several days, leaving out nothing, including his identity. Now was the time for trust and action—there was no other course.

"I've heard of you," Barlow said when Bolan was finished. "And admired you."

"People say I'm just a killer," Bolan said.

"In a small country like ours that is constantly besieged from every side we must all be killers sometimes. We have no armories in Israel. We carry our weapons with us. When the wars come, we fight where we stand."

"Life and death," Bolan said.

"Every day," the black-haired woman said in English with a French accent. "My name is Judith Meyers. Sara and I were cousins. We both came here from France for education when we were teenagers and fell in love with the homeland. I . . . appreciate the burial you gave her.''

''That crane won't stay broken forever,'' Bolan said.

''We must stop it now,'' Nat Barlow said. ''We'll handle this our way, Mack Bolan. Thanks for all you've done.''

''No,'' Bolan replied. ''This is my fight, too. Maybe as much mine as yours.''

''Can you take orders from me?'' Barlow asked.

Bolan answered with another question. ''Do you have a superior in your government?''

Barlow smiled. ''Sometimes,'' he said, ''there are things that need to be done faster than governments can do them.'' He stuck out his hand. ''Welcome to Sabra, my friend.''

THE CRANE WAS BACK in operation as the Sabra agents moved casually toward the ship in ones and twos. There was no time for subtlety, especially now that the main deck rails were filled with swarthy men, all watching the dock and wharf. There would at least be no problem now with making sure this was the right ship. They'd know just as soon as they tried to board.

Bolan walked with the ex-New York City cop turned freedom fighter, the two warriors sharing an understanding only they could know.

''We'd had some vague warnings about this from our other agents,'' Barlow was saying. ''When Sara disappeared and didn't check in, we knew something was up, but we didn't have enough information to act. We've had soft probes on the wharves all week, but this has been too smooth to get a fix on until you stumbled upon me this morning.''

"I've never stumbled on a cop in my life," Bolan said. "The eyes give you away every time."

"You mean you fed me information?"

The Executioner nodded. "When I saw you this morning, I knew I had to set up some sort of contact or we'd have ended up with a three-way fight."

Barlow snorted. "No wonder they haven't caught you yet."

"Yeah," Bolan said. "Staying alive's a full-time job."

They reached an old Ford flatbed truck backed up on the dock. One wooden crate was already in place in the back of the vehicle, another just then swinging over the edge of the *Latva*'s deck to be lowered. The driver, an Arab with a large, black mustache, was out of the truck, helping to direct the lowering.

"We'll start here," Bolan said, his K-bar knife in hand. He bent quickly, slashing a front tire, then moved around the other side to get that one.

He stood, the creaking of the crane covering the hiss of escaping air. They moved up near the gangway.

"They'll be waiting for us," Bolan said.

Barlow reached into his jacket, taking the safety off his Uzi machine pistol. "I wouldn't have it any other way. Ready?"

"Any time you say."

They moved to the gangway, hitting it at a brisk walk, six other Sabra agents coming up behind, with Johnny and Judith Meyers taking up dock positions to clog escape routes. If the boat was what Bolan thought it was, they were all walking into a firefight in which they'd be seriously outnumbered—but no one complained. Silently they walked, all of them ready to do what justice called upon them to do. Like the dead woman in Palm Beach, they were soldiers of the night, fighting their lonely battles outside of the public eye.

It didn't take long to answer all the questions.

There was shouting on deck, and when Bolan saw the first glint of sunlight on the barrel of a carbine, he was running, the MAC-10 in one hand, the Beretta in the other.

He hit the main deck on a dead run, diving and rolling as rifle and machine-gun fire shattered the peaceful morning, thousands of wharf gulls screaming into the hazy sky.

They were everywhere, swarming the deck, Arabs and greasy American hoods, all armed to the teeth with the best technology Uncle Sam could muster.

Bolan rolled to a crouch, firing from the hip, driving the enemy back with covering salvos that got the rest of his squad on deck. Then the killing began.

With reflexes quicker than thought, the Executioner raked the top of a huge wooden crate marked Fragile that sat beside the open cargo bay, taking off the tops of three heads that fired from behind, bone and brain exploding in instantaneous death.

He spun, men charging from all sides. He finished the clip with two one-second bursts, the parabellums taking the legs right out from under several of them, heaping them atop one another in screaming agony.

"Get cover!" Barlow yelled from behind, as his people fanned out in an ever-widening circle, its interior a safe zone.

From the upper decks, hoods with M-16s fired from the rails, dropping one of the Sabra agents, his arm torn off by the shells.

The Executioner looked up. As the deck angrily splintered all around him, Bolan used the 93-R in controlled 3-shot bursts. Isolating himself from everything but his targets, he punched through six of them, one after another, all killing shots to the upper torso. The bodies tumbled over the rails above, falling to the deck like human rain, their weapons clattering down with them.

A Sabra agent ran the deck and jumped to the crate that was still suspended from the crane. He climbed atop the now wildly swinging box, using a knife to slash the rope holding it to the cable. He landed on deck with the crate, its sides splitting, M-60s and boxes of ammo spilling out along with the television sets that were supposed to be inside.

Barlow ran to the rail, pointing down at the truck and yelling. "That one! Get that one!"

The driver was already taking the truck out of there, his vehicle swerving erratically as he tried to drive on the rims of his front axle.

Johnny and Judith ran to the center of the dock, opening up with their stutterguns. Civilians scrambled for cover as the pavement sparked under the friction of the parabellums. The truck covered fifty yards before the crate on the back caught fire, then blew seconds later with a deafening roar.

The concussive effect of the blast threw the driver through the windshield, the rolling truck careening sharply to the right, plowing into Barlow's snack stand before the gas tank erupted in orange flame. Both truck and stand went off the edge of the dock and into the Mediterranean, leaving behind a residue of oily black smoke.

They had the enemy on the run. The deck had cleared of all but bodies, as everyone retreated under cover.

Bolan ran to the hatch to follow as Barlow hurried up to him, a combat grimace frozen on his face. "How many do you make?"

Bolan ejected the clip from the Beretta, jamming another clip into the butt. "Ten or fifteen," he said. "How many we lost?"

"Two," Barlow said, taking a deep breath. "Ready?"

"It's your party."

Barlow swung out with the door, opening to a barrage from the narrow passages within. He came around with the Uzi, emptying the whole clip into the hallway, driving the enemy back. Bolan followed the fusillade into the acrid, smoke-filled hall.

A head poked through a doorway and tried to withdraw. Bolan drilled a third eye. He ran to the place, charging into a dining room filled with enemy guns. The Executioner knocked over a table for cover as M-16s opened up. It was steel, heavy enough to withstand rough seas, bullets singing loudly as they ricocheted off its dull top.

Barlow and several others followed him in, grabbing cover where they could find it. Flaming hell existed for thirty seconds as everyone emptied their guns at once in the large room.

Bolan held back with the Beretta. When the initial volley subsided, he stood without cover and took out the enemy soldiers one at a time, blasting mechanically wherever they were exposed until the clip ran dry.

Then the gunners charged, swinging empty rifles like bludgeons. The K-bar was in the Executioner's hands and he came up under a swinging rifle as another Sabra agent fell. Bolan thrust the knife into a terrorist, going for bone. The fighting was close. He came up, aiming at a throat.

Then it was over.

Three Sabra agents stood knee-deep in bodies. They were breathing heavily, blood and gore covering them from head to foot.

"Gather our dead," Barlow ordered, and a second later one of the female agents poked her head in the door.

"Some of them are down in the hold!" she said. "I think they're trying to blow it."

"Get the bodies!" Barlow yelled. "Let's get out of here!"

Bolan was already racing for the exit, heading for the deck. He had no idea how to make it to the hold other than from above.

He cleared the hatch into sunshine. Barlow's people were busy getting their dead and wounded down the gangplank.

The hold lay exposed before him, a large square hole that dropped fifty feet in the deck. There were still a great many crates left—how many had already gone? Several men were down there scurrying around the wooden boxes. Nobody had fired on them for fear of shooting into live ordnance. Bolan had no such fear.

They were setting small charges of C-4 with timers to give themselves the chance to get away. Bolan saw three of them, crouched in different sections of the hold.

The Executioner shoved another clip into the 93-R and stiff-armed it out in front of him.

"Bolan, let's go!" Barlow screamed from behind.

He didn't respond, instead firing at a Mafia man, taking out the guy's kneecap. To be certain, he put one in the other leg.

"I can't move!" the man screamed to his partners. "Don't set the timers!"

Another mafioso stood, ignoring the danger and digging for hardware. Bolan finished him with a round in the chest.

"No!" the downed man screamed. "Please!"

He swung to the third man, an Arab, who continued to work on his charge without stopping. Bolan put one through his leg, too. But it didn't work with this guy.

"Bastard!" the man screamed and finished setting the charge. He began laughing then, high-pitched, hysterical laughter.

Bolan turned and ran.

The Sabra agents were already hurrying down the dock to safety. Only Barlow awaited him at the base of the gangway.

Then Barlow glanced over his shoulder, pointing back toward the ship. "Look!"

Bolan followed Barlow's finger to see two mafiosi coming down the gangway with their hands in the air. Barlow leveled his Uzi and started back for them. "Let's take these guys," he said.

Bolan stood his ground. "Nat!" he ordered. "Stop!"

But Barlow was already squeezing his trigger, stitching the unarmed thugs, who rolled the rest of the way to the dock.

Bolan's face twisted with rage, and he ran back to the Sabra agent. "We could have used them for information!"

Barlow's reply was lost as the freighter blew then, erupting apart in a series of rumbling explosions. The first concussions sent the warriors facedown to the dock, which threatened to go as it shook madly, cement pilings crumbling beneath it as huge sections fell into the sea.

The sky turned orange, then white, as the air itself seemed to be ripping apart, smoke billowing away, pushed by a gentle breeze. The wooden roof of the wharf caught fire, dry timber turning the area into a raging inferno all around them.

And just when it seemed everything would be swallowed up, it was over. The rumblings stopped, the dock half gone. Sirens wailed plaintively in the distance as Bolan rolled over to dust himself off. The *Latva* was gone, totally and absolutely.

10

The Sabra headquarters was located on a tree-shaded cul-de-sac on Rambam Street in the heart of the ultraorthodox Jewish quarter of Haifa. Its front was a *mikva*, a ritualistic bath, the continual ebb and flow of traffic disguising the presence of agents.

Nat Barlow and Mack Bolan sat across from each other at a large dining table; a nearby doorway led to a small kitchen. The room was large and open, furnished with many chairs. Books were piled everywhere. There were no windows, but TV screens monitored every angle outside.

Several cots were set up at the far end of the room, and except for the gun cases set in the cinder-block walls, there was no ornamentation. A small group of agents sat tensely around the room, speaking in stage whispers.

A telephone rested on the table between the two warriors. They were engaged in the part of warfare that combat veterans hate the most—waiting.

"Isn't there something else we can do?" Bolan asked. "I hate sitting here while those guns get into the wrong hands."

"Everyone I can spare is out running his contacts," Barlow replied, lighting another cigarette on the butt of the one he had been smoking. The ashtray beside him was filled to capacity.

"Through the whole country?" Bolan asked.

Barlow took a long drag, exhaling slowly. "Fortunately, it's a small country, about the size of, say, Massachusetts. You think they'll use some of the explosives soon?"

"It's logical," Bolan said. "The longer they keep stuff around, the better chance of it getting discovered. From the tone of Metrano's letter, I think we're in for some heavy-duty problems—and soon."

"What 'Zionist landmarks' do you think he was talking about?"

"You live here," Bolan replied, taking a sip from the dark, bitter coffee that sat in front of him. He shook his head. "You tell me."

"This is the land of the Bible," Barlow said. "The whole country's full of landmarks...though I would suspect that Jerusalem would have to come under attack at some time. They can go after both Jews and Christians there at the same time."

Bolan thought about that. The PLO had one aim alone—to conduct the war of fear. Believing Israel a land meant only for them, they waged jihad—holy war—against the unbelievers, meaning Jews and Christians. Considering it their divine duty to slay infidels, they used whatever methods struck the most terror in the hearts of their enemies. That meant war on innocents, wholesale slaughter of children in elementary schools or the bombing of hospitals. And whatever else the Executioner thought about this, the overwhelming sense of guilt and responsibility overrode it all. Why wouldn't the phone ring?

"Does your oganization have any official status?" he asked Barlow.

The man shook his head. "We're sponsored by several members of the Knesset, our parliament, and funded by donations of American Jews through the Jewish Defense League, but like you, we must have the freedom to act immediately in emergency situations. Israel is technically at war with eighteen surrounding Arab states. Things happen too quickly to rely on politicians."

JOHNNY BOLAN AND JUDITH MEYERS stood in the kitchen, finishing up the dishes from lunch and listening to the exchange between Bolan and Barlow.

"I'm sorry about your cousin," Johnny said, when there was a temporary lull at the dining table.

Judith looked at him, her eyes a pale blue, her face lean, but somehow soft looking. "I think we all expect it in this business," she said, a catch in her voice, "but Sara and I were children together." She laughed, caught herself. "We used to routinely run away from home together. I guess I just . . . I just . . ."

She broke down slightly, turning her head from him, sniffling. He felt awkward, then ashamed of his awkwardness. He put a hand on her shoulder. She turned and slipped into his arms, letting him comfort her. "Sara had so much life in her," she said. "So much...desire for life. She was the one who wanted to join Sabra when we heard about it through some army friends. She wished desperately for the land we love to be free from pain, to know the peace that would allow everyone to enjoy life."

Judith moved away from him then, slightly embarrassed. She took a deep breath, composing herself. "Now she'll never know how things came out. She died on foreign soil, not buried among her own kind."

"Funny," he replied. "Sometimes I feel that way about my brother."

She wiped her eyes on the back of her hand. "What?"

"You should have seen Mack before...when he was younger." Johnny turned and looked through the open door to make sure no one could hear him. Barlow was across the room, trying to read a book, while Bolan stood nearby, watching the outside monitors. "He was always happy, always laughing. When I was a kid, I idolized him. Life meant so much to Mack. Nobody could have a time like he could."

He finished drying a dish and put it up in the cupboard, closing the wooden door. "Then came the war, and the deaths of the rest of our family. Mack stopped being my brother and became something else, something a lot darker. Sometimes I don't know him. Sometimes I don't think he knows himself."

"Combat changes people," Judith replied, and she turned to look at Bolan through the door. "It can scoop out the sensitivity and just leave the empty shell. I've seen it happen. We worry a lot about that here because of the nature of what we do. That's why we're called Sabra. The sabra cactus is hard on the outside, but soft and sweet to the taste on the inside. We must not lose our humanity, no matter what. I fear that perhaps your brother has crossed the line."

"I fear it, too," Johnny said, surprised to hear those words coming out of his mouth. He had not even dared think them before.

Johnny quickly changed the subject. "How come all of you speak English so well?"

"It's required in all the schools," she answered. "Since we come from so many places, it tends to be a common ground for most of us. Plus, we owe a great deal of our continued existence to our friendship with the United States. We...appreciate our position."

The phone rang loudly, making both of them jump. They moved to the dining room door, watching both Barlow and Mack run for it, Bolan waiting for Barlow to pick it up.

"What?" Barlow said into the phone. "Just a minute." He got out a small pad and began writing. "Got it," he said after a minute. "I'll be in touch."

He hung up the phone and looked around at the expectant faces that crowded in on him. "We've made some of them," he said. "Right here in town."

11

The Dan Carmel Hotel perched on the summit of Mount Carmel, the entire city spread beneath it down the mountainside. This was the highest point of the port city. A Turkish cannon still sat on the hotel grounds, pointing out over Haifa to commemorate the last outpost to fall when General Allenby took Israel from the Turks in 1917.

But for Mack Bolan, the Executioner, the Dan Carmel was more than a scenic hotel with a history— it was killing ground, and very poor killing ground at that.

Now he stood with Barlow, Johnny and twelve other Sabra agents on the darkened grounds. They were staring at a bulbous projection from the second floor of the hotel, called the Le Rondo, a fancy French restaurant that boasted the best view of the night city. According to Barlow's intelligence, a mysterious American had rented the restaurant for the night, but had insisted on bringing in his guests via the outside, emergency-exit stairs that were normally closed to the public, instead of through the hotel itself.

In the hours following the destruction of the *Latva*, this had been the best lead the Sabra people had come up with although there had been movement. Every business and person under Sabra surveillance had been on the move. The energy in the air was electric—tonight would be yet another night of horror for Israel. Unless the Executioner could do something about it.

Officially, the government was listing the destruction of the ship as an unknown quantity under investigation. Unofficially, all covert branches of the Israeli military had been mobilized for action.

"Thoughts?" Barlow whispered around him in the darkness.

"We must limit the fighting to the restaurant itself," Judith said. "This is a tourist hotel. A gun battle in there could have international repercussions."

"Agreed," Barlow said. "My feeling is to take half our force and go in through the hotel entrance, making that the least likely route of escape. We'll spread the rest up the outside stairs and on the surrounding grounds."

"I disagree," Bolan said. "The hotel entrance is down a long, narrow hallway that could easily be defended by two guns. If you force them through the windows and the outside stairs, you'll need most of your firepower right out here."

"International publicity is a major concern for us," Barlow said. "Our survival as a country depends a great deal on the goodwill of our allies. We can't take the chance of letting this leak into the hotel."

Bolan nodded. He didn't like it, but until he could come up with his own sources of information, he'd have to play by Barlow's rules.

They split up into teams, Johnny part of the squad of three who would defend the outside stairs that spiraled from an emergency door in the center of the building. For the most part the place sat on stilts, twenty feet above ground level, and three more men waited in the darkness beneath the building to catch anyone coming through the windows.

Bolan moved through the remnants of forest that occupied the back of the Dan Carmel toward the well-lit front. He was dressed in combat gear down to his harness, as were the rest of them. Barlow hurried to catch up to him, and they entered the light together.

The lobby was bright and wide open, with a long counter on their left as they walked in. The room's atmosphere charged instantly, employees and guests looking in shocked surprise at the six men armed with submachine guns who hurried past them.

At the counter, Bolan saw an employee frown deeply, then reach for the house phone in front of him. The Executioner realized immediately how the place had gotten rented that night. He ran to the desk, flashing out with a hard right hand to level the traitor before he could phone and warn his cronies upstairs.

The man fell to the floor, his head cracking on the key cabinet behind him.

Bolan jogged to catch up with the others, who had taken the series of small flights of stairs leading up to the hallway that exited only at the Le Rondo.

There was one way to play this one, fast and loose. Move quick and hope the element of surprise was on your side. Surprise was the warrior's best friend and worst enemy, depending on whose side it was on. Bolan knew they'd need all the help they could get tonight.

Barlow stationed a man at the far end of the hallway to keep anyone from wandering in accidentally. The rest of them moved quickly toward the double glass doors fifty paces away.

They were a third of the way before the man with the M-16 on the other side saw them. He turned to shout as Barlow emptied the Uzi pistol into him, shattering the glass at the same time. The volley's impact hurled the gunner against a wall behind, then he bounced back onto the jagged shards of glass that still poked up from the metal door frame.

Seconds later, they were running across his body and into the round restaurant. Barlow left two more men at the door, three enemy guns out of commission now, and they charged in and hit the jackpot.

The room was swarming with PLO, all dressed in black. Knapsacks were on the tables. And there was a virtual orgy in progress. There were nude women, coupling frenziedly with the terrorists. Forbidden liquor was everywhere, the smell of hashish strong, its haze hanging like a cloud in the room. Bolan saw

Family there, too, recognized Big Tommy's son, Guido, and several of his buttons.

Everyone froze for a second, like people posing for a photograph. Bolan took it all in at a glance and knew what they faced. Like the laughing man on the *Latva*, these were special troops. This was a taste of heaven for Muslim fighters: the women, houris, mythological nymphs; the drugs and alcohol, nectar of God. Like the Society of Assassins during the Crusades, these men were experiencing the afterlife in advance so that they'd be prepared, even hopeful, they would die. These were suicide troops.

The lull lasted only an instant. Bolan cut loose with the MAC-10, trying to take out Guido first. But the man was already moving, dumping over his table and diving for the floor, literally scores of people charging between them.

Someone hit the lights, plunging the restaurant into darkness, only pale light from outside giving any definition at all. Pale light and the staccato flash of a room full of stutterguns that gave everything a surreal, strobe-light effect.

Sabra had the better ground. Several men charged their position, but were unable to attack in force because the room narrowed near the doors, allowing only one man through at a time. Still they tried to come in waves, presenting easy targets for Bolan's MAC-10.

Gunfire sounded from outside as they tried the emergency exit, but only death waited on the stairs.

The clamor of the guns was deafening, the dark room a shooting gallery with only the screams of the women punctuating the reports of the weapons.

Bolan and Barlow were positioned on either side of a doorway. "What the hell is this?" Barlow yelled, as he shoved another clip into his Uzi pistol.

"A training session," Bolan returned, "on the use of plastic explosives!"

"The knapsacks?"

"Yeah!"

Three terrorists came for the doorway, and Bolan took them out with 3-shot bursts. They fell on top of one another like firewood, their bodies piling up to form a natural wall.

The crash of breaking glass was interspersed with weapons fire as tables were hurled through the remnants of the large plate-glass windows that surrounded the restaurant. They were going out the hard way, just as Bolan figured. Now Barlow's plan would have to stand the test.

The men in black grabbed knapsacks and began leaping out of the windows all around. Gunfire could be heard on the hotel grounds as the terrorists dispersed with their deadly packs, shadows jumping in the night.

Bolan moved into the doorway, firing over the wall of dead that lay piled before him. He aimed high, heads exploding as the bodies slumped back onto dining tables. But even the Executioner couldn't be everywhere at once. They were escaping into the night, and there weren't enough troops outside to stop them.

Fifteen feet away, one of the wounded terrorists rose painfully from the pile of dead, his hands in the air. As Bolan raised the MAC-10, a hand pushed it aside.

"I want this one alive," Barlow said. "We need information." He stepped over the bodies in the doorway to bring the man in. It was then that Bolan saw the knapsack hanging from the man's arm.

"Nat, no!" he called, then dived aside reflexively.

The force of the blast shook the whole restaurant, all the glasses in the bar breaking, large sections of ceiling falling in.

Bolan was around the door frame, and the explosion missed him completely. The other Sabra who had defended the doorway with them wasn't so lucky. He lay on his back, a gaping hole in his chest. As for Barlow, there was not much to find. His head lay on the floor beside Bolan, the eyes still open wide in wonderment.

Bolan jumped back to his feet, grabbing the Uzi from the hands of the dead man beside him. He waded over the dead, moving in frenzy mode into the restaurant itself.

Most of the terrorists either were dead or had escaped into the night. Those who remained soon enough learned the lesson of Bolan's justice.

He moved through the room and took them out one at a time. The Uzi became an extension of his body.

But there was method to it. He was marching inexorably toward Guido Metrano's table.

The room was quiet by the time he neared Metrano's position, except for moans rising above the carnage. He stood five feet from the overturned table, scoping for signs of life.

All at once, Guido rose from the debris, an M-16 in his hands. Face frozen in a death's-head grin, he pulled back the trigger on full auto at the same time Bolan did.

Hot pain seared the Executioner's shoulder, but it was as close as Metrano ever got. The Uzi chopped him nearly in half, his dead fingers clamping hard and emptying the rest of his clip into the ceiling before he hit the carpet for good.

Guido's heels were still drumming on the floor as Bolan hurried to him and searched his pockets. He found money and a small map case, both of which he took.

It was his show now—*he* had the information. He spared a thought for Barlow. The Sabra agent had failed, not because he wasn't a true warrior, but because he had underestimated the enemy.

Mack Bolan would never make that mistake.

12

At precisely 10:00 p.m., two BTR-40 armored vehicles rumbled along the mountainous stretches of Lebanon's Highway 2. They were rapidly approaching the well-defended border checkpoint at Rosh Hanikra.

The vehicles were armed with Russian 7.62 mm SGMB submachine guns, and the terrorists who manned them were itching for action.

The man known only as Abba sat behind the wheel of the second vehicle, his mouth tightening to a grin when he had visual sighting of the crossbars and sentry boxes.

On his left rose the hills of Lebanon, on his right, several hundred feet below, the Mediterranean Sea crashed against the rocky shores, relentlessly carving out the limestone grottoes this area of the country was famous for.

This was it, he thought, the phalanx of the thrust that would bring the Jewish nation to its knees. At exactly this moment, all over Israel, his people were striking fear into the hearts of the infidel through coordinated suicide attacks on populated areas.

The second blow, the destruction of their holy places, would come tomorrow night. But tonight he and his people would occupy Palestinian soil again. Tonight they would drink the hot blood of victory on the enemy's home territory.

Troops were rushing into the road ahead, first shouting, then raising their rifles and firing. And Abba was happy, for killing brought him more pleasure than sex, more pleasure than anything. And killing Israelis was the greatest pleasure of all. He laughed out loud as the BTR bounced over the mangled bodies of several soldiers.

The first armored vehicle crashed through the border checkpoint, the flash of gunfire all around it illuminating the night. Abba was right behind, his gunners tearing hell out of the border patrol. Just inside the checkpoint, the barracks that housed the Israeli troops exploded, sending wood debris splintering in all directions like wooden rain. Abba was pleased. The foot soldiers who were crossing the border with him were doing their job.

Troops came running out of the demolished structure like human torches, their bodies aflame. Abba laughed as one tumbled off the edge of the highway, falling two hundred feet to the sea below.

The carrier in front careened to the side of the road, tumbling on its side, tires still spinning. It partially blocked the roadway, men climbing straight up to get out the door that was now above their heads.

There was no time to stop. Abba hit the tail end of the lead carrier at full speed, hurling it off the road, throwing the occupants violently out as the gas tank exploded in orange fury.

He had made it. The few troops left at the checkpoint were being taken out by his infantry. To his left, he saw several hundred more of his people running toward the hills, crossing fully armed into Israeli territory. The warnings had probably gone out, but that didn't matter. His men didn't have far to go.

TWO CARLOADS OF SABRA AGENTS hurried away from the carnage at the Dan Carmel. They had lost six of the twelve who had done battle at the Le Rondo. They had to leave in such haste that this time they weren't even able to carry off their dead.

Mack Bolan, the front of his skinsuit soaked with blood from a superficial wound to his shoulder, sat in the passenger seat of the white Fiat. Judith Meyers, a distant look on her face, negotiated the winding hill road like an expert. She was mumbling to herself in Hebrew. Johnny sat in the back with a red-haired man named Hillel, who had taken a bullet in his left shoulder and was hunched up against the door. Behind, the other car cut off and took a different road. They would meet back at Rambam Street.

The gloom in the car was palpable. They had failed. Sabra had lost an able leader, and though they had killed some of the suicide troops, many more had escaped into the night. This wasn't the PLO's only rallying point, but it was an important one.

Bolan had Guido's information in his pocket, but hadn't had time to figure out any of it yet. One thing he knew for sure: those people tonight had been dressed for action, and at this point there was nothing he could do about it.

He thought sadly about Barlow. In many ways the man had been like the Executioner, like what the Executioner had once been. The very thing that had made him real, though, his humanness, had been his downfall. But maybe, Bolan thought bitterly, there were worse things than being dead. Like his personal war. Would it ever be over?

No time now to ponder his mortality. He looked at Judith. "Who's in charge?" he asked.

She turned to him blankly. "Please...not now. I'm saying kaddish for the dead."

"There'll be more dead...a lot more, if we don't get ourselves together quick."

"Nat Barlow was our heart and soul," she answered. "He had no chain of command. We all followed him out of love."

"Someone needs to take charge."

"He's right," Johnny said from the back seat. "How many people can you get to the streets if you have to?"

"Twenty-five," she answered, gearing down to take a sharp turn. "Maybe thirty."

"Can we get them quickly?" Bolan asked.

"How quickly?"

As if in answer to her question, a huge ball of white-hot fire rose from the harbor far below them, the sound of the explosion reaching them a second later. One of three oil storage tanks on shore had exploded. The second and third went in unison seconds later, the brightness of the explosions lighting the whole city to near daylight.

The body counts were already being bannered over the television screens when Bolan and the Sabra survivors straggled into the *mikva* headquarters a short time later.

Video scenes of devastation ran before their eyes like some ghastly reminder of the Holocaust: the oil storage tanks destroyed by men in cars, who blew themselves up with the tanks; the waterfront museum's front torn out by a human bomb during a well-attended lecture on ancient sailors; the Haifa Gardens blown to pieces; the Knesset building in Tel Aviv heavily damaged by a human bomb who charged into the lobby, blowing himself up before a statue of Golda Meir; Ben Gurion Airport heavily damaged by human bombs; six Leumi Banks of Israel destroyed and looted; the whole east wing of the King David Hotel in Jerusalem demolished. The list was endless, the death toll already reaching more than a thousand.

The news reports sobered Mack Bolan. Despite everything he had done, which had been considerable, still enough of Big Tommy's blood chit had made the streets to knock the wind out of an entire country. And Bolan had a feeling it wasn't over yet. Having taken Israel's bodies, the PLO now would go after its soul. The "Zionist landmarks" referred to in the intercepted letter still hadn't gone up, and it was on these that the Executioner would have to concentrate. His job had just begun.

He put a hand to the superficial wound on his shoulder. Guido Metrano's hot fire had come within a millimeter of ending the Executioner's everlasting war once and for all. Instead, Guido lay on a table somewhere now, a slab of meat, and the Executioner still walked. What Fates had decreed that slight tremor of Guido's hand that enabled Mack Bolan to continue his lonely crusade? Perhaps that was what kept him going—destiny.

He looked around the room. Everyone was busy. The wounded were tended; the combatants cried together for their country, and consoled one another, urging strength and courage to go on. Even Johnny had become one of them in their struggle.

Bolan did not miss the attraction between his brother and Judith Meyers. Even now they sat together at the dinner table, sharing the closeness of an emotional bond. But no one came near Mack Bolan. Though his cause was just, he was Death to them, cold and unfeeling.

He couldn't stay in this place, he knew that. He'd have to go back to Acco, to his safe house, and study the map case he had taken from Guido's pocket. No one knew he had it yet, and at least for a while, he wanted to leave it at that. So far, working with Sabra had caused as many problems as it had solved. He might need them later, but right now he wanted to figure things out on his own.

The killing on the streets had died down; all of it had appeared to happen in a fifteen-minute period around 10:00 p.m. He figured it to be over for a while, the enemy using the lull to build up fear for the next attack.

He was tired, hurt and sick at heart. And for the first time in his long fight against the forces of the night—he was confused.

A bad, perhaps deadly, combination.

THE ROSH HANIKRA KIBBUTZ squatted barely a mile within the border. Known for its orchards and gardens, it was one of the showplaces of modern Israel, a successful cooperative whose men, women and children lived full lives of peace and happiness.

It was a choice and prime target.

Abba and his henchmen hit the gates of the kibbutz at full throttle, the BTR pounding through the wood and metal in a rending scream, several hundred PLO troops pouring in behind.

Abba watched happily from the cab of the BTR as his troops overpowered the meager opposition the people of the kibbutz offered. They were gunned down in the yards between the long wooden houses and other buildings that made up the compound. The houses were then quickly surrounded to stop any of the survivors from escaping.

The terrorist leader observed a brief firefight in the wide courtyard near the broken gates, the infidels taking out a number of his troops with concerted fire.

The battle wound down quickly, then Abba climbed out of the truck to issue orders.

"Gather the dead," he called. "Pile them up and burn them. Then put all the survivors in two buildings, men and women separate. You may have your way with the women, but don't kill them. They will be hostages to ensure the safety of our new headquarters."

He watched his troops spring to action, nodding his approval the whole time. Holstering his pistol, he took a deep breath. It was good to breathe Palestinian air again. It was very good.

JOHNNY BOLAN SAT with Judith Meyers at the long table, a piece of honey cake uneaten in front of her. He studied her closely, watched her mentally steeling herself against the pain and horror that kept trying to surface.

"You should eat something," he said.

"Time enough for that," she replied, staring straight ahead at the wall. "We have much to prepare for."

"Let it out," he said. "Let yourself grieve for just a little while."

She looked at him then. "I can't," she said, and took his hand in both of hers. "I must be the strength of my people. Ours is a history of betrayal and persecution. Our race has survived intact for four thousand years, and always the world has wanted us dead.

"When Hitler tried to exterminate us all in the death camps, the whole world turned their backs. When Great Britain divided Palestine into Jordan and Israel in 1948, we were forced immediately into a war to protect our new country, and we fought it alone. We fought the Six Day War and the Yom Kippur War—all alone. We are surrounded by nations who live only to crush us under their boots. If we're not strong—if I'm not strong—they will wipe us all out. We love life, but must wallow in death, for there is no one to stand up for Israel."

"I will," Johnny said softly.

Her lower lip quivered, and she fell easily into his arms, sobbing quietly. "I think that God has sent you to me, Johnny Bolan," she whispered.

"Can I borrow a car?" came a hard voice, and they broke the embrace to see Mack Bolan standing, frowning, beside them.

Judith wiped at her tears, taking a deep breath. "What's ours is yours," she said, and took the Fiat keys out of her pocket, handing them to him. "Is there something we can help you with?"

"No," he said. "Johnny and I have some business to take care of." He put the keys in his pocket. "We'll be in touch. Let's go, Johnny."

Johnny Bolan stared at his brother, at the hardness in his eyes, then looked at Judith. She was purposely keeping her expression blank, not wanting to interfere between the brothers. But he knew what she was thinking anyway.

"Give me a minute, Mack," he said.

The Executioner nodded and moved to stand a discreet distance away from them.

Johnny took her hands, kissing one, then the other. He was amazed at the contrast—so strong, yet so soft. Sabra. "I don't know what Mack has in mind," he said. "But this won't change anything."

She nodded, not believing him. "Don't let him harden you," she said.

"Mack's all right," Johnny replied. "He's just...I don't know...."

"Crazy," she said.

Johnny shook his head. "No...no, he's not. He's just...seen too much, that's all. We'll be back soon. I know we will."

"Let's go!" Bolan called from across the room.

She leaned over and kissed him on the cheek. "Take care," she said softly.

"I'm not sure where we're going," he said into her ear. "Wherever it is, I'll send word."

They pulled away from each other and Judith nodded, her blue eyes looking fragile as spun glass. Johnny got up and walked across the room, feeling all the while like a deserter.

13

Mack Bolan sat on the edge of his bed in the dark and read Guido's maps by the penlight he held in his mouth. Across the small room, Johnny lay quietly sleeping on the other bed, and that was the way Mack Bolan wanted it.

He had avoided working within structures for a long time now, because of precisely what happened at the Dan Carmel hotel. This next step he'd take on his own. It wasn't so much that he didn't need help at this point, especially his brother's help, but more that he didn't feel he could trust any but his own feelings.

Johnny was tied to Sabra through Judith. That was fine, but in an emergency, he didn't need to be faced with divided loyalties. Sabra's goals were above reproach, their methods commendable, but Bolan was sufficiently familiar with Middle East politics to know how it operated.

Terrorist groups launched mortar and rocket attacks on Israeli territory from Lebanon, Syria and Jordan; the Israelis organized a counterstrike in which they captured hundreds of PLO prisoners and jailed them in an old Turkish prison right down the ocean drive from Acco; since the captives were prisoners of war, they could legally be held indefinitely, so eventually the government of Israel turned them loose to begin the process all over again.

The Executioner didn't operate that way, and he wasn't going to this time. Maybe he was wrong, but a lot of scum were no longer around to terrorize and prey on the innocent because Mack Bolan had meted out swift justice. He wondered how many of those causing havoc right now had come under Israeli guns before. Better that Johnny sleep through this one while Mack Bolan did some permanent mopping up.

And it looked as if Guido Metrano was going to provide the key. The man's effects had included three maps of Israel, all marked off in grids. The first map showed three meeting places where, apparently, the PLO had established forward bases. One was close to Haifa, in the Yizre'el Valley near Atula. One was in Kfar Saba, northeast of Tel Aviv. The third was in Tel Aviv itself, near Clore Park, right on the beach.

On this first map were references to the other maps, with grid marks written in sequence. On checking the second map, Bolan was able to pinpoint the locations of the attacks that had come tonight, plus from what base they had been launched. From his cursory examination, he could see what good his operations had already done, for barely half the prescribed targets had actually been hit.

Then he came to the last map. Its grid marks matched up to the first map also, except these targets had not been hit at all, yet. These were the targets for the next night.

JOHNNY LAY IN BED feigning sleep, watching his brother. He was planning something, Johnny was certain, but whatever it was, Mack had decided to remain secretive about it.

Johnny watched as Mack stood and peeled off the skinsuit he still wore, changing silently into street clothes. Then he went to the makeup case. Johnny stared in fascination as Mack skillfully darkened his hair and skin tone, adding a mustache and black-framed glasses as a final touch. He looked like an Arab now.

It made Johnny angry that Mack had kept information from him—and from Sabra. Wasn't this *their* home? He'd seen many good people go down today, and it seemed like a hell of a time for Mack to turn into the Lone Ranger.

His brother shouldered his duffel and moved silently through the door.

Johnny hopped out of bed immediately and slipped into his shoes. Whatever happened, he was going to be there for it.

BOLAN MOVED OUT of the room and into the dark hallway. He checked his watch, and the luminous dial showed 3:00 a.m. The downstairs bar was closed now for the night, the whole place asleep except for him.

He moved quietly down the hall, then downstairs and into the bar itself, lit softly by a small neon sign advertising a local beer.

A phone sat behind the bar. He found it easily and used his penlight to find the numbers while he dialed. He couldn't do this one totally alone, but at least he could control his end of it.

Judith Meyers, voice tired, answered after the fifth ring.

"There's a house," he said without greeting, "near the south tip of the Kfar Baruch Reservoir, five miles from Atula. Take your exterminating equipment and you can kill some vermin."

"Where will you be?"

"I'm keeping busy. You'd better hurry."

"*Toda*, Bolan," she said. "Thanks. Is Johnny—"

He hung up the phone, cutting her off. He slipped quietly across the rough wooden floor, the front door opening easily. The Fiat was parked around back.

FROM THE TOP OF THE STAIRS Johnny heard his brother replace the phone receiver, then listened as he left the bar. He rushed down the stairs and made it to the front door just in time to see the Fiat cruise quietly around the building, its taillights etching a path to the front gates of the walled city.

He opened the door, running into the hot night. Very few people in Acco could afford cars, and most of those were hobbled with metal locking devices on the front tires. He frantically ran the narrow streets until he found an unfettered car.

He climbed in and hot-wired the ignition of the small Datsun. Mack had no more than a few minutes' head start. He'd catch him soon enough.

THE GATES at the Rosh Hanikra kibbutz were damaged beyond repair, so Abba simply blocked the gate by piling up several cars from the compound end to end and side by side. He now stood on the kibbutz side of the makeshift gate, a teenage boy held before him, the barrel of his pistol jammed against the youth's temple.

On the other side of the barricade, an Israeli colonel named Wolfson stood at parade rest, his mouth fixed in a scowl, his eyes traveling from Abba to the boy and back again. Behind the colonel, several thousand Israeli troops stood with weapons ready, prepared to repay in kind the horrors visited upon their families and friends by the PLO.

"We have 253 Jewish sluts and bastards in those buildings over there," Abba said in English, pressing the barrel a little harder, the teenager wincing in pain. "If you don't pull back, we will begin killing them one by one."

"Don't be ridiculous," the colonel said. "You'd pay for such an act immediately. All of you would be dead within minutes."

"We do not care," Abba said.

"Listen to reason. You leave now, simply cross back over the border, and that's that. We won't follow. All we want are the hostages."

"Then pull back."

"How far?" Wolfson asked.

"Two miles. The border and the crossing will be ours."

Wolfson's lips tightened to a hard slash. "I'm not authorized to do that. It's not our policy."

Abba nodded, smiling. "I understand. I will give you something to tell your superiors. Ma'as!" he called loudly.

A soldier in olive drab appeared and Abba's face turned dark and sullen. "I just want you to appreciate *our* position, Colonel," he said loudly, then turned to the soldier. "Take out your gun."

The man unholstered a long-barreled .38.

"Good," Abba said, nodding broadly. "Now... shoot yourself."

Without a second's hesitation, the man raised the gun to his temple and pulled the trigger, gore splattering all the way to where the colonel stood.

"Our points are nonnegotiable, my friend," Abba said. "You must make your decision now."

Revulsed by the senseless act, Colonel Wolfson turned immediately to face his troops. "Fall back to the base camp!" he yelled, and walked away without looking back.

14

Arab settlements in Israel were always easy to spot—they all contained large numbers of television antennas. Being surrounded on all sides by Muslim countries, Muslim residents in Israel watched the television broadcasts from these countries to remind them by just how large a margin they outnumbered the Israelis.

Bolan used these antennas as a beacon, driving slowly into the Arab settlement near Kfar Saba. It was a small city of stone houses, the foundations millennia old. There was only one place large enough to house that many people here—the firehouse.

The firehouse was set in the center of town, a two-story structure of wood built in the early fifties. It served the entire area surrounding Kfar Saba. It was by far the newest building in the town, the next oldest a thousand years its senior.

Bolan left his car on the outskirts of town, hidden in some bushes off the main road. Eliminating all but essential items from his duffel, he then hoisted it over his shoulder and began the quiet walk through the darkened streets.

No one disturbed him as he picked his way around the small stone dwellings, an occasional dog barking, then quieting when he passed. When he was within a block of the fire station, he knew he had the right place. A lot of cars were parked around the structure, more than this village could support, and he saw three . . . no, four guards with automatics stationed all around. He'd have to take them first.

Without hesitation, he dropped the duffel in an alley near the station and put on his best drunk face. He staggered out of the alley and took to the middle of the street, humming loud enough to be heard by the guards without rousing anyone else.

He watched them congregate as he neared the structure, their rifles at the ready. He hummed a bit louder, opening his arms wide, then turned a full circle. He did this twice, then fell on the ground in the middle of the dirt road.

As he struggled to his feet, now thirty feet from the guards, he could see them poking one another and pointing, their laughter drifting across the open expanse of air to him. Good.

He staggered on toward them as if oblivious to their presence. They were calling to him gently, so as not to awaken those within. He didn't understand a word they were saying, but moved around toward them, mumbling. He was itchy for it, his hand going back to reassure himself that the K-bar was still stuck in his belt.

They were totally at ease as he moved within striking distance, smiling wide, rolling his eyes. They laughed and joked with him, obviously poking fun. The Executioner nodded dumbly, then stumbled, falling against one of them.

The knife flashed, and he came up quickly, burying it in the dark man's heart—one down. He jerked the blade free and turned on the others before they realized anything was wrong.

Like a released spring, he jumped at the other three, leaving the knife in one guy's throat, knocking the other two to the ground. Before they could yell, he stuffed a fist full of dirt into the first one's mouth, leaving him choking while throwing his weight on the remaining man.

The man writhed beneath him, and Bolan's right fist crashed into the guard's jaw. He whimpered and lay still. The sentry's M-16 had fallen beside them. Bolan grabbed it by the barrel, then brought the butt around in a wide swing. The weapon slammed into the side of the other guard's head, causing the man to spew out a mouthful of sand. The blow sent the sentry crashing to the ground.

Bolan turned to the other guard. He was on his knees, trying to pull the knife from his throat. The Executioner jumped quickly to his feet, ready for anything.

The terrorist was crawling now, blood running in thick gobs from his severed jugular, soaking into the sand beneath him. Bolan watched him without feeling, waiting for the life to seep out of one who didn't deserve it.

Seconds later, the man fell, sprawling, trying to crawl. Then he flopped onto his stomach, everything oozing out of him in a long sigh.

Moving quickly, Bolan dragged the men up near the cars parked around the structure, pushing the bodies one at a time beneath the vehicles and out of sight. Then he ran quickly across the street, retrieving the duffel and bringing it back to the station with him.

He figured that what he had to do wouldn't take long. He moved into the shadows, then dipped into the bag. First he drew on a pair of rubber gloves. Next, he removed a hundred-foot length of rope he had for scaling walls. He then pulled out dynamite, blasting caps and detonator, finally getting the wire cutters.

He worked quickly, first cutting any phone lines to the outside world. He set several charges around the structure, tying them all in at the hand detonator, which he strung across the street.

He took the length of rope and moved to one of the cars, unscrewing the gas cap. He fed the rope into the gas tank, soaking it through. Then he pulled out the wet rope, stringing it from car to car, gas tank to gas tank, looping the rope into each tank before moving on to the next car, finally ending the length right atop one of the charges.

He looked at his watch. It was 4:00 a.m.

He grabbed the duffel and ran across the street, pulling out the Ingram MAC-10 as he ran. A light flared on the second floor, a silhouetted figure moving to the window to watch him. He heard voices from the building—yelling.

He reached the detonator just as the first of the semiclad men came running out of the fire station. He quickly bolted down the leads and twisted the detonator handle, the sound of feet pounding on the roadway loud to his acute hearing.

The dynamite went up with a roar, then the gas tanks in quick succession, all of it happening within seconds. The entire end of the street exploded in orange fire, the station igniting like dry tinder. Flaming bodies leaped screaming from the windows.

Bolan moved into the street, which was as bright as day around him, burning cars scattered everywhere like children's toys. The heat from the blaze seared his face. He gunned down the two or three people who had escaped the explosions, then triggered a few mercy rounds into the flaming ones.

Another explosion ripped through the structure as the gas tank on the fire engine blew. Then the whole building collapsed into a pile of rubble, fifty-foot flames licking the night sky.

He hesitated for a heartbeat to make sure they were all dead, then he picked up his duffel and jogged back to the Fiat.

"WHAT DO YOU MEAN, he's dead?" Big Tommy growled into the mouthpiece of the field telephone.

Jamil Arman answered in that soft, nerve-jangling voice. "Your son Guido gave his life tonight so that the revolution might live."

"Where's his body?" the mafioso asked, his insides churning. "I got to see the body."

"Unfortunately that is not possible. The Israeli authorities have cordoned off the whole area of the hotel."

Metrano looked around the living room of Arman's underground bunker. Everyone was asleep but him. If that son of a bitch Jamil had just given him his money and let him go, Guido would be alive right now.

"Where are you?" he said. "Where's my money?"

The man chuckled. "I am nearby," he said. "We have pushed into Palestine and set up our forward base. You will have your money when you come to join us."

"You're insane!" Metrano shouted, several of his men stirring in their sleep. "I came here to sell you some goods, not get involved in a fucking revolution."

"But you *are* involved, my friend. Don't you understand that?"

"I understand that two of my boys are dead and I'm out ten million bucks because of you. Where's Tony?"

"Your other son is safe."

"What the hell's that supposed to mean?"

"You promised us professional help in demolition. He is in Tel Aviv right now, providing us the help you so graciously promised."

"And you promised me ten mil."

There was a slight pause, then Arman said, "And you may have it. I am sending someone to pick you up and bring you here to our headquarters. At the celebration tonight, I will give you your money."

Metrano picked up an unlit cigar stub from an ashtray nearby and stuck it in his mouth, chewing. "Listen, my *friend*. I want my money and I want it now. Then I want to take what's left of my people and get the hell out of here. Get it?"

"I understand your words."

"So have someone bring the money."

"No."

"What do you mean, no?"

"You've heard my conditions."

"I'm warning you...."

"I know," Arman said softly. "You can...sue me."

Tomasso Metrano thought for a minute, realizing just how smart Arman was. By involving Big Tommy in every act of warfare he committed, he was tying their fates together directly. Metrano could never go against the man on any level, lest he risk sharing his fate.

"There's something else, too," Arman said. "I know who killed your son."

"Yeah?"

"An American dressed in black who walked through the restaurant firefight as if he were immune to bullets."

"Bolan," Big Tommy said, practically spitting the word. "Can we take care of him?"

"Of that I have no doubt."

"Good. Get that car over here. I'm ready for you."

15

Johnny Bolan stood on the stairs leading down to the beach and looked at his watch. It was 4:30 a.m. Tel Aviv, a city of raucous activity, was at its quietest. As usual, his brother's timing was impeccable.

Johnny was halfway down the stone stairs, his head just poking up to street level, as he watched the Executioner across Herbert Samuel Street, preparing to enter the old Arab hotel through its street-side open-air café. Behind him, the waves rolled gently in to the long expanse of beach.

A mile farther down, the four-thousand-year-old port of Jaffa jutted boldly out into the ocean, its stone Crusader and Turkish buildings and Muslim minarets still intact. The Phoenicians had used the port, as had Jonah. It was where the cedars of Lebanon had been brought in for Solomon's temple.

Johnny moved up another step to get a better look. Tel Aviv was a metropolitan city of cafés and late-night parties, the entire length of the beachfront street jammed with restaurants and coffee houses. There would be no explosions here like those he had witnessed in the other place—too many innocent lives,

too much innocent property at stake. If Mack needed
him, it would be here.

He had seen Mack take care of several guards, and
could see him at that moment fitting the silencer on
the muzzle of his MAC-10 and jamming extra clips
into his belt.

Johnny shook his head in disbelief. Maybe Judith
was right. It was just plain crazy to go in there alone—
suicide. Even Mack couldn't hope to overcome the
odds on an operation like this. He couldn't let him go
in alone, he'd have to—

Suddenly hands grabbed him, pulling him backward down the steps. Without control he fell hard, his
head hitting each step until he lay at the bottom.
Through the pain and the haze that blurred his vision, he could see men staring down at him. He recognized one of them. Tony Metrano.

"Welcome to hell, asshole," Tony said.

THE EXECUTIONER TOOK a deep breath and reached
for the door handle, quietly using a key he had found
in one of the dead guard's pockets. The key fit easily,
the door creaking open on rusty hinges.

The building was narrow and three stories tall. He
figured there were about thirty men inside. It would be
one of the most difficult assaults he had ever at-
tempted. But if he handled it right he could do the job
and get away clean. He'd start on the top floor and
slowly work his way down, trying to take them out in
their sleep as much as possible. His success depended

almost entirely on his getting away from the top floor undetected. If he couldn't, then getting out of the building would pose its own set of problems. He thought of this in passing, but didn't dwell on it.

He started in the door, but was startled by the sound of his own name. He swung quickly to the source across the street, his MAC-10 ready, his body in a combat crouch.

"Look what I got," came Tony Metrano's voice.

Bolan looked, and his stomach did a sluggish barrel roll. They had Johnny. Two Mafia buttons held his brother by each arm, Tony standing behind with the muzzle of a .45 automatic buried in his neck.

"You got about a second to drop the hardware, soldier," Metrano said loudly, "or they'll have to take away the rest of this clown with a street sweeper."

Bolan could hear activity in the building behind him, people on the move. Johnny looked dazed, unable to support himself. Blood ran from his nose and mouth.

"Take me instead," the Executioner said. "No hassle. Just let him go."

"I got both of you." Metrano smiled back. "Drop your iron, now!"

They had it, the chink in the death man's armor. Countless times since he had let Johnny run with him, he had wondered about this moment, knowing somehow, someday, it would have to come. The one light that brightened the cold, lonely place where his soul lived was being snuffed; and while he stood hard as a shadow on the outside, his insides were screaming. The Executioner, whoever he was, whatever he had become, did indeed have a heart—and it was breaking right now.

He should have bolted. He should have tried to take out Metrano and hope that Johnny was coherent enough to keep up his end.

Instead he dropped the MAC-10.

To die in Tel Aviv. Why not? Nobody cared anyway.

They were pouring out of the building behind him, rough hands grabbing, pulling on him, taking the rest of his weapons.

They punched him, but he was already too numb to feel. They hurried Johnny across the street and dragged them both inside the restaurant.

And the brothers were swallowed up by the building—no witnesses in the early morning, no help on the way, no cards up the sleeve. It was just the two of them, and a gang of people who would enjoy nothing more than taking their lives whenever they chose. Slowly.

Something hard clipped Bolan behind the right ear, lights dimming all around him without the bliss of unconsciousness. Time moved in jumps as he was dragged upstairs and thrown roughly to the dirty floor, Johnny dumped on top of him like a sack of fertilizer.

He remembered feet, then searing pain as he was kicked repeatedly by steel-toed boots. Then he and

Johnny were jerked upright and pushed into a couple of wooden chairs. Bolan felt the ropes being wound around his body as he was bound to the chair.

For a few moments they were alone. In a haze he could make out his brother, head leaning to one side, also roped down.

Bolan sat uncomfortably in the semidark room, his head clearing by degrees. He craned his neck to get a look around. It was bare except for several now unoccupied bedrolls. The windows where covered by brown paper, so he couldn't get an idea of what floor they were on. He tried to recall how many flights of stairs he had been brought up, but couldn't. So, he assumed they were on floor three. Too high to jump.

Johnny sat beside him, blood and spittle smeared on his face.

"You okay?" Bolan asked.

Johnny stared, his eyes still a bit foggy. "I'm sorry, Mack," he said. "I only wanted to help, I . . ."

"Forget it," Bolan said. "What we've got to do now is figure out a way to keep on living."

Johnny forced a smile; his teeth were bloody from where he had bitten his tongue when he tumbled down the stairs.

The Executioner began to work his chair toward a window. He tried to stand but, because of the ropes across his thighs and lower legs, found that he couldn't. He thrust his head forward and gripped an edge of the brown paper with his teeth, then inched his way across the breadth of the window.

The paper ripped slowly, revealing bars beneath the glass. Great. Now the best he could do would be to try and break the glass. Then what?

The door flew open, Tony Metrano filling the space. Seeing Bolan at the window, he snarled loudly and moved over there, grabbing him by the hair and pulling him away, chair and all.

"Don't even think about it," he said.

Bolan saw the man's fist arcing toward his cheek, and he grimaced, anticipating the blow. The pain was fierce anyway, leaving a ringing in his head. Then Metrano bent and grabbed one leg of the chair. He gave it a sudden jerk, and Bolan crashed to the floor.

"Leave him . . ." Johnny started, but was silenced with a slap across the mouth.

Tony stood between the two of them and began to talk, his face angular and mean looking beneath well-groomed curly hair.

"You're in the wrong place at the wrong time, fellas," he said. "You killed two of my brothers and tore hell out of the business my father has worked his whole life to build. That don't set good with me, you know?"

He laughed and took out a cigarette, lighting it slowly, savoring the moment. The room was dimly lit, early-morning sun beginning to filter through the rip in the window's paper covering.

"I'm gonna do you bad, both of you. I ain't gonna kill you yet, cause my pop wants to do that himself.

But I'm gonna do the next best thing. I'm gonna make you *wish* you were dead.''

He leaned toward Johnny's face, blowing a long stream of smoke, making the younger Bolan cough. "Thought you guys were so smart. When we heard Guido was dead, we figured you'd show up here.''

"I've already told everything I know to the government,'' Bolan said, trying to maneuver the chair to an upright position. He succeeded after a few moments.

Tony turned to him, angry. He grabbed his hair, jerking his head up. "Now I don't like that!'' he said loudly. "You're a lying son of a bitch.'' He fired a punch into the back of Bolan's neck. "Somebody made you here already, and the government checked you out through Interpol and they figure *you're* the one who done everything. You've been all over the news. Rich, huh?''

He laughed again, turning back to Johnny. "You know, Pop only said to keep your big brother here, alive. He didn't say nothin' about you. Maybe I oughta knock you off first, so Hero Boy over here can know what it feels like to lose a brother. What do you think about that?''

Bolan's rage was barely controlled, but he kept it tight. "I think you're scaring us to death.''

"Oh, yeah?'' Tony took the cigarette out of his mouth and touched it to Johnny's face. "Like that better?''

"What the hell do you want from us?'' Bolan said through clenched teeth.

"Pleasure," Tony said. "A great deal of pleasure." He took a Swiss Army knife out of his pocket and flipped out the corkscrew. "I don't know as much about this stuff as Abba, but this is one kinda thing where on-the-job training can be fun and rewarding. For instance, do you have any idea of the possible uses for the eight blades in one of these babies?"

Bolan just stared at him.

He jabbed it into Bolan's arm and began twisting. "Let's discover together," he said.

16

Judith Meyers squatted in the brush one hundred yards from the old army barracks and waited. She wore camouflage, her hair tucked up under a black beret. An Uzi was strapped on her back; a Galil .223-caliber gas-operated automatic rifle was mounted before her, its tritium-lighted night sights flipped up to best advantage in the dark predawn haze.

Twenty-five of her people were ranged around the outpost that had served as housing for troops protecting the reservoir during the Yom Kippur War in '73.

She was worn out, physically and emotionally, and her stomach was knotted from waiting. They had called into the barracks, given the terrorists within the opportunity to surrender—and nothing had happened.

For fifteen minutes they had been waiting, as the dark sky turned slate-gray with hints of blue around the edges, and the reservoir behind the barracks began to quietly reflect its surroundings. But so far they had been greeted by absolute silence.

She heard scrambling in the brush near her, and turned her head to see Hillel, arm in a sling, making his way toward her. He carried a Desert Eagle .357 Magnum in his good hand.

He squatted beside her, staring toward the old wooden structure in the distance. "We've got to come to some decision," he said.

"I know," Judith replied. "Are you sure they can't be sneaking out on the lake side?"

Hillel shook his head, frowning. "No boats over there," he said. "Besides, we've got the waterline well covered."

She looked at him, saw her own lack of command experience mirrored in his young face. "We've got no choice then," she said. "I think we should give them five more minutes to come out, then we go in."

Hillel jumped up immediately, glad someone had taken the responsibility. "I'll tell Asher," he said, and moved off into the undergrowth.

Judith, alone again, thought of Johnny. She worried about him when he was with Mack Bolan. It seemed as if the elder Bolan faced death carelessly, recklessly, like someone ready to die. The Executioner could easily get himself killed and his brother right along with him. Johnny seemed to her so sensitive, so... vulnerable. She hated to see him wasted on his brother's death wish. One so dead, Judith thought, comparing the two men. One with so much to live for. She feared that if Johnny stayed with his brother for too long, he too, would die inside and become nothing more than an executioner.

She heard the roar of a jeep starting up, watched Asher drive into the clearing near the barracks. An M-60 was mounted on the back of the jeep; her friend Sylvie was manning it.

Asher stood on the seat and called to the terrorists in Arabic, giving them the deadline. But before he even got the words out, a man dressed in black appeared in the doorway, his hands raised high in the air. He was followed by others, all throwing down their guns as they stepped outside.

She heard a few seconds of cheering from the units on her left, then some left cover, hurrying toward the barracks to help process the prisoners.

Asher turned back toward her, waving, smiling wide. But Judith Meyers wasn't happy. She was beginning to appreciate the responsibility of command. The other terrorists had been bombers, prepared to take death to themselves like a new lover. Why should these be any different?

She picked up the binoculars that lay beside her on the ground, squinting to get a good look in the half light. She stood—and then she saw. Knapsacks. They were all wearing the knapsacks.

"No!" she screamed, waving her arms. "No! Make them strip before they come out!"

Asher had turned in her direction, a hand to his ear to try and make out her words. She ran partially into the clearing, everyone turning to her, and watched it all happen in slow motion.

The first terrorist had reached the jeep, and screamed in Arabic, "There is no God but God, and Muhammad is his prophet!"

Then he lowered his arm.

The man exploded in a huge fireball, and the jeep was picked up and tossed by the force like a toy. Asher was thrown clear; Sylvie was crushed under the machine before it exploded, spewing metal frags in all directions.

The terrorists charged then, screaming like devils, blowing themselves up as they neared Sabra positions. Their planning was simpleminded and direct— war of attrition. They were charging the Israelis in order to kill them all. If any of their people escaped the conflagration, they could carry on with their mission.

Judith dived back for the Galil, lying prone to fire. The landscape was a nightmare of bombs with legs, going exactly where they could do the most damage.

People were exploding around her, literally tearing to pieces. She saw a laughing terrorist grab one of the Sabra women in an obscene embrace, both of them going up, arms and legs flying like projectiles.

Cold fury took possession of Judith's mind. She began firing at the ones still coming through the door, aiming at head level, as screams and explosions assaulted her from all directions.

In control now, she eased back the trigger, taking off the face of a terrorist in the doorway. He fell

backward into the barracks, quiet for a second before
his charges went off, blowing the roof off the building in three large pieces. His explosion was followed
in rapid succession by others, as the human bombs still
left inside detonated.

With the burning rubble as a background, she could
see the charge of those still left outside. They were still
running, screaming, across the open ground, going for
the handful of Sabra agents still in hiding.

Her people were firing from four or five protected
positions in the trees, trying desperately to take out the
maniacs before they could cross the ground to them.

Four of them were coming under Judith's gun. She
got one just appearing around the hulk of the jeep, his
explosion shifting the wreckage again. Three still ad-
vanced, close enough now to distinguish faces.

She took the legs out from under one, and as he
sprawled to the ground he exploded, dirt and flesh
shooting twenty feet into the air, leaving a large crater
behind.

The Galil ran dry, and she jumped to her feet, un-
slinging the Uzi and folding out the stock. Explosions
ranged all around her; screams were piercing as one of
the Sabra positions was breached and destroyed.

Judith fired from the hip at the two remaining terrorists rushing at her. They were closing from no more
than forty yards, near enough to see their wild, staring eyes.

She got the lead runner with three short bursts, the
rounds demolishing his head. The last came charging

through the residual smoke from the first, and as she turned the Uzi on him, it jammed tight.

The fire in her brain threatened to consume her. She couldn't move fast enough, throwing down the Uzi and grabbing another clip for the Galil. Hands shaking, she dropped to the ground and ejected the magazine. The man was almost on top of her.

She fumbled one in, jamming it to click into position, and he was there, right there!

From a squatting position, she tried to grab the weapon, tumbling backward in the process, her finger locked on the trigger, stitching a line from ground level right up to the sky.

She took him with a diagonal line, blood spurting across his torso, throwing him backward from five yards distant. She rolled onto her stomach as he went up, his body popping with a loud thud.

And then there was quiet.

The Sabra agent rolled over, her own body and the area around her slick with blood and shimmering intestines. The man's arm lay beside her, the image of a scimitar tattooed just above the wrist.

As she stood shakily, those left from her company moved tentatively from their positions, surveying the carnage with disbelieving eyes.

Judith moved into the clearing and wondered if the Executioner would have lost so many troops had he been in charge of the expedition.

She stared at the sky, which was now brightening considerably. It was Friday. Sundown would mark the beginning of Shabbat, the holiest day to Jews, a time for rest and celebration. She knew this fact would not be lost on the terrorists, and feared that there was more horror planned before Shabbat was over.

She was convinced that Mack Bolan knew what that horror was. She had to find him and make him tell her what was going on. And she had to find Johnny.

Johnny.

ABBA WALKED into the Rosh Hanikra courtyard with Jamil Arman and Tomasso Metrano, feeling the excitement pumping him higher and higher. The troops cheered, shaking their M-16s high in the air, while the TV cameras of the world recorded the scene in the early-morning light.

Big Tommy kept trying to cover his face and look away from the cameras. "Jeez," he said. "Did you have to let the damned news people in?"

"This is a glorious day for our people," Arman said, waving to the cameras. "We rejoice in the recapture of even a small part of our beloved homeland. We take pride in our accomplishment."

"We are not common criminals," Abba said, looking at Metrano with disgust. "We are heroes."

Metrano fixed him with hard eyes. "Most of the common criminals I know wouldn't stoop to killin' women and little kids."

"Israelis are not human beings," Abba said. "They are bugs to be squashed."

"Yeah?" Metrano said. "And what am I?"

"Our ally," Arman said, too quickly. He smiled with his mouth but not with his eyes. "Come, Abba, we must send you on your way."

They moved past the cadre of reporters and cameras, off into the maze of kibbutz buildings. Next to one of these was parked an English Ford.

Abba opened the car door, but Metrano stopped him before he got in. "Remember," he said, "you tell Tony that I want these creeps alive until I can get down there and take care of them. Jamil's gonna arrange some safe transport for me later. I'll take my vengeance like in the old country, with my own hands."

Abba stared at him without speaking. He climbed behind the wheel of the car, Arman bending to the open window. "I want you to lead the operation tonight," he said in Arabic. "It's the only one left after losing the other bases. But if this one works out . . ."

"It will," Abba said. "I pledge my life on it."

"Good." Arman patted the top of the car and took Metrano by the arm. "Come, my friend. If it will please you, we'll return to my quarters by the back way."

"Now you're talkin'," Metrano said, turning to stare once more at Abba before walking off.

Abba started the car and drove off. It was all he could do to keep from spitting in Metrano's face. Americans were all soft, squealy pigs wallowing in their own shit. He wanted them all to die, and he knew exactly where to start.

Metrano wanted Bolan alive, but that would never happen. Of all the people Abba had seen on the urban battlefields of the Middle East, the Executioner was the most dangerous. To allow him to live even one second longer than necessary was worse than stupid. No, as soon as he got to Tel Aviv, Mack Bolan would die.

And that would be the end of that. Just another dead American.

He pulled up to the gates and honked, his men hurrying out to move the cars that blocked the exit. He then drove out the dirt road, bumping onto the main highway.

The Israeli army checkpoint blocked the road two miles away. According to the back-off agreement, two of his own troops also manned the checkpoint, and he was allowed through immediately, his passage radioed back to Rosh Hanikra by his people.

He was free, traveling the interior of Palestine unmolested. Still, he traded vehicles three times before finishing his journey to Tel Aviv.

17

The Executioner was no stranger to pain. In Nam, and in more places than he cared to remember. His body was a road map of his exploits, perhaps the only lasting reminder of how much he had truly given.

He sat next to Johnny, the harsh light of day brightening the brown paper on the windows. Watching the windows was the only way Bolan could measure the passage of time, for in the place where he took his mind, there was no such thing as time.

Tony Metrano had worn himself out torturing the Executioner. Now, Mack Bolan willed his mind to conjure up images of a beautiful family life that existed only in his memory. As the painful aftereffects of physical abuse were trying busily to drain him of any humanity he had left, he was thinking now of a world of peace and freedom, justice in the land that had given him birth. Those were the ideals that kept Mack Bolan alive, that gave him the strength to carry on. And, yeah, it was worth it.

They were waiting through a lull in the torture. Tony, anxious to do it all himself, was resting and having lunch. Bolan had taken most of the abuse.

Usually taciturn, he had become talky and insulting when Metrano had started on him. He figured that if he could keep Tony angry enough at him, the man would leave his brother alone. It had worked. It was the least he could do.

He took stock of his faculties. His face was a mass of welts and cuts, swollen, he was sure, beyond recognition. One of his eyes was shut, his hearing impaired in one ear. Nothing major seemed broken, although Metrano did not seem to have missed any part of his body. But his muscles were tight, his system in peak condition. The knife had done some mean work, and blood trailed from many places, but basically Tony was afraid that too much abuse would kill the man, depriving his father of the pleasure.

Bottom line—the Executioner was still in working order except for the pain. And in Mack Bolan's life, the pain was a given, anyway.

"Mack?" Johnny said weakly.

Bolan turned to look at his brother. He tried to smile, but couldn't manage it. "Guess I lost that round," he rasped.

"You don't look so good," Johnny said, trying for a smile. "Are you . . . are you . . . ?"

"I'll live," Bolan replied, then tried to laugh at his own joke. It came out a racking cough. "How about you?"

"I hurt, Mack," Johnny said. "But my legs still work. I could run. If only . . ."

"We're not through yet," Bolan said, though he didn't know if he believed it. "Hang in."

"Yeah."

There was silence for a minute, and Bolan knew that Johnny had something he wanted to say, but couldn't get out.

"What is it?" the Executioner finally asked.

Johnny looked at him, his eyes misted. "Did you . . . come here to die?" he asked.

Bolan swallowed painfully. He could sure use a drink of water. "I can't answer that," he said.

"Can't or won't?"

Bolan slowly shook his head. "I don't know the answer. I sometimes think that maybe I've been looking for death for many years. Sometimes I think I'm . . . already dead."

"I'm not ready to die," Johnny said, as if the statement could alter their predicament.

And the Executioner felt the weight of even more responsibility. Had he thought of everything? Was there something more he could do?

He heard the door opening, a tiny squeak drawing his attention. There stood a dark man in black. He wore a light windbreaker, and Bolan could see that it covered a shoulder holster. The man's eyes were evil, cold and hard as stone.

"We meet again," he said softly, and smiled without humor. He walked right up to Bolan, leaned forward in front of his face. "Do you remember me?"

"Florida," Bolan said. "You were there at the house."

"You got away from me that time," Abba said, and drew the MR 73 out of its resting place. He took the silencer out of his pocket and began screwing it on. "This time we end the game for good."

Bolan's thoughts raced. If he didn't do something fast, both he and Johnny would be dead within thirty seconds. Big Tommy wanted the Executioner for himself and wouldn't care to have someone else horning in. That was why the man was being so quiet. Before Abba had finished putting the silencer on his gun, Bolan had reached a decision.

"Tony!" Bolan screamed. "Tony! Help! Help!"

"Stop!" the man ordered, whispering harshly.

Johnny took the hint and started screaming, too. Abba hurried with the silencer and had just aimed his revolver at Bolan's head, when Tony burst through the door.

"Abba!" he said, pulling the man away. "What the hell do you think you're doing?"

"Getting rid of your trash," the man returned, trying to jerk himself from Tony's grasp. "Get your filthy hands off me."

"No!" Tony said angrily. "These two are for my father to handle."

"You must take care of them now, while you have the opportunity. They are dangerous."

He was right, Bolan thought. They shouldn't be able to hold him.

Tony wrestled Abba's gun away, and shoved him back against the wall. "We'll do this the way my father wants," Tony said. "We'll wait."

"He cannot get away," Abba lied. "He asked me to take care of it for him."

"He would've told me that," Tony countered.

"He could not call, the phones are out."

"What?"

"He asked me to take care of this matter for him," Abba said. "I am only trying to help."

Tony faltered, looking at the gun in his hand.

"Try the phones," Bolan said. "He's lying."

"Shut up!" Tony screamed at Bolan, pointing the weapon at him. "Or I'll save my father the trouble."

Abba was reaching for the gun. "Now if you will just..."

"No," Tony said. "I want to try and call my father first."

"Are you calling me a liar?" Abba asked.

Tony brightened. "No. I just figured that maybe the phones are working now."

The two hoods glared at each other, and Bolan realized that a punk was a punk no matter where he came from. Let the two scorpions eat each other alive.

"We'll call together," Tony said, and held the gun loosely, but pointing in Abba's general direction. The man got the message and moved out the door.

They argued loudly as they walked away, and because the others in the house were all Abba's people,

Bolan couldn't predict the result no matter what happened.

It was time to make a move.

"What now?" Johnny said.

"Now we get out of here," Bolan replied. "I have a plan, but I'll need your help."

The Executioner worked his chair over to the nearest wall, then with the tips of his toes began to push himself into a rocking motion. On the third backward movement, he fell to the floor.

"Mack! What are you doing?"

"You'll see. Move your chair over to the wall with the back against the wall for support. Then I'll roll over so you can jam down on one of the chair legs with your feet."

Johnny quickly got the idea and followed his brother's instructions. At first he could not exert sufficient force because of the strictures against his legs. Finally, after three tries, they both heard a muted *crack*, like wood splitting. The sound echoed in the room as if a gun had been fired. Or so it seemed to Bolan. At once his head swiveled toward the door, and he hoped that no one outside the room had heard it too.

One agonizing heartbeat later, Bolan rolled onto his back and began to move his legs up and down. Soon the chair's leg began to move inward, under the seat. Bolan could feel his bindings loosening. He worked at it some more, wriggling constantly, then turned onto his stomach. He moved his shoulders, then his arms up and down. Finally the rope fell away and he slipped his arms out.

He was free!

He stood, shaky for a moment after his constrained position and the effects of the torture he had suffered at the hands of Tony Metrano. But the Executioner was free.

He untied his brother, then helped him to stand, supporting him under one arm.

Mack Bolan had built his resolve to incredible proportions to achieve his freedom, and now all that resolve turned to deep and unquenchable anger.

It was time to kick butt.

18

Mack Bolan's shirt was hanging in bloody tatters from his pain-racked arms.

"Come on," he said.

"I can't help, I'm still . . ."

"Let's go," Bolan said, his voice intense. "I'll carry you if I have to."

Johnny recognized the directness of Bolan's thinking—and perhaps his anger. It was useless to argue or to plan. He shut his mouth and moved near the door, scared to leave, scared not to. It was all up to Mack now.

Bolan stood glaring at the closed door, breathing deeply, prepared. He took two steps backward, then bracing himself against the pain, threw his two hundred pounds behind the rush, splintering the door off its hinges.

They found themselves in a hall beside stairs that wound down two flights, turning back on themselves landing after landing. The stairs formed the center of the small building and were wide open.

An Arab guard stood wide-eyed in the corridor, staring at Bolan as if he were a demon from hell.

Bolan snatched the M-16 out of the man's hands, then shoved him through the railing that separated the hall from the open stairwell.

The man fell, screaming, landing with a sickening thud on the ground floor. Mack grabbed Johnny and immediately began helping him down the stairs as excited voices came to them from the rest of the building.

They made it almost to the next landing before the stairs were swarming with men. Bolan was ready. In fact, he was anxious.

Bolan opened up with the M-16 at full auto. He took out three of them at chest level, driving the others back.

The two brothers reached the landing, Bolan blasting the first door he came to. The lock shattered, and the thin wood paneling splintered under the onslaught. Two more dead men lay behind it, sprawled on their backs.

He pulled Johnny across the bodies to the next flight of stairs, people now firing at them from above, forcing them against the wall. He stitched the stairway overhead; another body dropped past them to fall atop the other a floor below.

They were halfway home, but the going was getting rougher.

The terrorists charged through the doors in groups. Bolan had enough ammo left to fire a short burst in front and behind, and then they were on him from two sides.

Unable to shoot without hitting each other, they went for him barehanded. He backed Johnny against the wall and flattened against him as they came on. He swung the rifle until he broke it, then he went after them, flailing away with fists and kicks at the never ending stream of men who came for him. And even as he fought, he and Johnny inched farther down the stairs, trying to make the second-floor landing.

Someone got a hand on Bolan's throat. He leaned forward and pulled his assailant over his head; the man somersaulted in midair over the railing, bouncing a few times before plummeting to the first floor.

Then a gunshot echoed the halls, an Arab falling away from Bolan, others jumping aside. Abba stood farther up the stairs, smiling, smoke curling from his MR 73. He was going to take out the Executioner even if he had to kill all his own men to do it.

Everyone backed away, and Bolan did the unexpected. He charged.

He closed the distance between him and Abba in a second, surprise still on the man's face as Bolan grabbed him and threw him to the next landing.

Then Bolan threw himself down the stairs, hitting several terrorists while still in flight, his momentum making them fall on top of others.

Ten people hit the landing in a heap, Abba at the bottom of the pile. Johnny eased away from the wall and moved down nearer the landing.

Bolan wriggled to his knees in the pile, punching with combat-hardened fists at anything that moved. He saw Abba's face oozing blood.

Then Bolan jumped up, turning to see Tony Metrano one landing above, leveling a riot gun.

The Executioner grabbed his brother and threw himself through the rail, just as Metrano's shotgun blasted holes through the wall where they had been standing.

They fell hard, Mack taking the brunt of the impact to protect Johnny in the fall.

They had landed on two other bodies. Bolan rolled off quickly and regained his footing.

One man stood between them and the glass door that led to freedom. Bolan broke into a run, leaping into the air a few feet short of his human obstacle. The flying dropkick caught the Arab square in the chest, hurling him against the door, glass exploding with the impact.

Jagged shards of glass ripped the terrorist open in dozens of places; Bolan hoisted Johnny over his shoulder and plunged headlong into the hot, Israeli afternoon.

The streets were filled with people, thousands more jamming the beach across the busy thoroughfare, as the citizens of Tel Aviv prepared for the celebration of Shabbat. They stood openmouthed as a wild man, covered with blood, stormed into their midst carrying another man over his shoulder.

Bolan forced each step, pushing himself far beyond his limits. He had to put distance between them and Abba's people before he could rest, before he could let the exhaustion and the pain overtake him.

ABBA CRAWLED OUT OF THE PILE, yelling at his men. He looked up to see Tony Metrano coming down the stairs toward him.

"You imbecile!" he screamed. "I told you to kill him."

Metrano's eyes narrowed. "Watch it," he said. "I'm the one holding the gun."

Abba spit blood, his eyes wild, his face bruised and oozing red. He jumped to his feet and ran down the stairs, Metrano close on his heels.

As he ran through the café, he grabbed the M-16 dropped by the man sprawled just outside the door. He primed it, running out into civilization.

"Bolan!" he shouted. "Bolan!"

"No, Abba..." Metrano said, trying to get to him.

But it was too late. Abba opened up on the crowds, firing indiscriminately. Screaming and crying punctuated the staccato cry of the death machine in his hands. And as innocents piled up under the bite of the M-16, he added another sound to the mix—his own hysterical laughter.

"You're mad!" Metrano shouted at him.

"Yes!" Abba returned, and the gun, mercifully, went dry in his hands.

"We've got to get out of here!"

Abba ejected the magazine and ran back to the broken door. "My friends!" he called into the building. "Take to the streets! We meet in Jerusalem!"

He turned back to the death scene, smiling at the dead and wounded who lay like scattered leaves all over the street, the rest of the crowd still running.

"What about Bolan?" Metrano asked.

"Mr. Bolan will also meet us in Jerusalem," Abba said, slinging the carbine over his shoulder. "We shall settle all accounts then."

19

Mack Bolan, bruised and exhausted, hobbled the two blocks to where he had left the Fiat. Johnny was still slung over his shoulder; the burden made movement difficult, and the shoving, panicked crowds nearly knocked them over several times. But he made it, just as he had made it many times in the past, and he set Johnny down by the passenger door of the small vehicle.

Johnny sagged against the car, semiconscious since their fall down the stairwell.

Bolan hurried open the door. "You all right?" he asked, helping his brother into the car.

Johnny nodded. His eyes were glazed, but clearing. "Did you see..." he began, but Bolan cut him off by closing the door.

The warrior moved around to the driver's side. "I saw," he said through clenched teeth. "I saw."

Hundreds of people were still rushing past them, fleeing the pointless carnage at the hotel. Bolan, his key gone, hot-wired the ignition and slid through the crowds and onto Herbert Samuel, the sound of sirens already loud in his ears.

Several Israeli army vehicles rumbled past them heading toward the hotel, two-and-a-half-ton carriers filled with armed troops. He shook his head. They were probably looking for him.

His body was drained, his mind running in overdrive, on pure duty. He knew where Abba and his cannibals would be tonight, and he knew what they'd be doing. And he promised himself that their time was coming, bet on it.

Johnny half lay on the seat, an ugly black burn on his cheek from Tony's cigarette. He faced Mack, his eyes distant. "It was awful," he said in a low voice. "Old men, young girls in bathing suits—gone, just blown away for nothing. I saw a mother and two children...."

"Enough!" Bolan ordered, his own eyes dark. He glared at his brother. "If we don't finish what we came here to do, there'll be even more blood shed."

"Sometimes I wonder..." Johnny said.

"What, Johnny?" Mack said.

"I wonder about your feelings, that's all."

Bolan turned off Samuel and onto Ben Yahuda, heading for the coast road and Acco. "So be it," he said, surprised at Johnny's words, but conceding that perhaps Johnny wasn't thinking straight because of the abuse he had suffered.

They made the drive in silence, Bolan alert to the many army patrols they were passing. Yeah, he had feelings that ran so deep they threatened to drown him sometimes. But he needed to prove nothing to his brother or anybody else. A soldier couldn't surrender to self-pity and sympathy until the job was completed.

A savvy warrior couldn't afford to let any other emotions cloud his sense for war. He had to remain sharp, alert. He had to kill with precision or die himself. It was that complicated and that simple. If Johnny couldn't understand that about him after all this time, it was something he'd simply have to live with.

It was two in the afternoon when they arrived in Acre. Everything was quiet. In times like these, the Muslim population stayed off the streets, lest they get caught in the cross fire between the government and the terrorists whose feelings they didn't share.

Bolan drove down the narrow street, parking in front of the bar where they had rented the room. "Wait here," he told Johnny, as he moved to look in the front door.

The place was empty except for Braxis, the owner, who was sweeping up.

Bolan returned to the car, making sure no one was watching them before helping his brother out and hustling him into the bar. Then he hurried back to retrieve the duffel from the trunk, joining Johnny inside.

Braxis looked at them, his face darkening. "What kind of trouble do you bring me?" he asked harshly.

Bolan kept moving toward the stairs. "The kind I'll pay well to keep secret," he said.

"How well?" Braxis had laid his broom aside and was checking out the windows.

"A thousand dollars American," Bolan said, starting up the stairs.

Braxis locked the door and put out the Closed sign. "A thousand dollars will buy you one more night, no more." The man started pulling down window shades.

"One more night's all I need," Bolan said. "Can you help us get medical supplies?"

Braxis rubbed his stubbled chin, a smile slowly creeping onto his face. "For two hundred American dollars I can."

Bolan mustered a smile. "Fair enough. Come up when you're ready and knock three times."

Bolan eased Johnny onto the bed, then locked the door behind them. He went immediately to the duffels for artillery. His MAC-10 was lost to Abba's people. He replaced the MAC-10s from the duffels, shoving straight 9 mm clips behind the trigger guards. For a side arm, he took out a sleek Wilkinson Linda 9 mm, dropping on the bed the folding stock and 16 1/2-inch barrel that converted it to a carbine.

Johnny studied his brother from the bed. "Is it all over?"

"It's just beginning," Bolan said. "Tonight I take care of the rest of that scum."

There were three short knocks on the door. Bolan jumped, the pistol in his hands. "Yeah?" he said.

"It's me, Braxis," came the muffled reply. "I bring what you asked for."

"Are you alone?"

"Yes."

Bolan moved to the door, snapping open the lock and flattening himself against the wall, the Linda up and ready.

The door swung open. Braxis was standing there with towels on his shoulders and a basin filled with steaming water in his hands. A small bag of supplies hung from his arm.

He stepped in, raising his eyebrows when he saw the weapons. "I saw your picture on television," he said.

Bolan motioned him in. The man walked to the window casement to set down the water. "It wasn't me," Bolan said. "You must be mistaken."

Braxis turned and looked at him blankly. "You owe me $1,200. American," he said.

"I want to watch your television," Bolan said.

"One hundred dollars," Braxis smiled, holding out an open palm. "In advance."

Bolan returned to the duffel, producing a wad of bills. "More than enough," he said, handing the stack to Braxis. "Keep the change."

The man's eyes brightened, and he hurried out of the room for the television, returning with it in less than a minute.

"Food," Bolan said, taking the set. "Leave it by the door in the hall."

Braxis hurried out. This time he didn't ask for any more money.

"This place is dangerous," Johnny said.

"I don't like it either," Mack replied, hooking up the TV to a portable generator in the corner. "Though I don't think we'll be here much longer."

"We've got to rest, Mack."

"Tomorrow," Bolan said, and began washing up as the television came on.

News reports filled the Israeli channels. The reports were in Hebrew, so they couldn't understand a word, but the pictures told it all: the newsreel footage of the occupation of Rosh Hanikra, complete with shots of a shy Tomasso Metrano, scenes of the firefight at the Kfar Baruch Reservoir, the destruction of the firehouse, ending with the slaughter of innocents in Tel Aviv. All these shots were interspersed with pictures of Mack Bolan straight from the Interpol files.

The connections they had made to tie him with the terrorism were logical, though flawed. He was in the process of becoming an outlaw in another country. At that moment, he was probably the most wanted man in Israel.

He stared at his face in a cracked mirror hanging on the wall. His Arab makeup was long gone, washed away by blood and abuse. The swelling had gone down somewhat, but he could still barely recognize himself. The change had probably helped get him through the army patrols.

Methodically, he set about cleaning and dressing their wounds, his own body a mass of pain. Undoubtedly, the pain kept him from passing out from exhaustion. In that, it was his closest friend, for he had no intention of sleeping—not yet.

He worked on Johnny first, applying medicine and field dressings like an expert. "Where do you go from here, Mack?" Johnny asked, as a long cut on his arm was bandaged.

The word "you" was not lost on Bolan. "Jerusalem," he said.

"What's there?"

"The old city," Bolan replied, "King David's city. Abba and his...associates intend to destroy the Western Wall tonight."

"What!"

Bolan nodded. "The holiest place on earth for the Jews."

The Western Wall, also called the Wailing Wall, is all that remains of King Solomon's temple, which had once housed the Ark of the Covenant. The wall is massive, the foundation stones laid nearly three thousand years ago. Jews from all over the world go to pray at the wall, leaving their prayers in the form of messages stuffed into the cracks. It is the symbol of all that it means to be Jewish, an undying link to the Jews' antiquity and their hopes for the future. It is the heart and soul of a people. It is everything. Its destruction would be an irreparable blow.

"You must tell someone about this, Mack," Johnny said.

The Executioner had gone to work on himself, starting with his battered face. "No," he said. "This one's mine."

"Sabra, at least, has a right to know."

"Especially not Sabra," Mack said. "You saw the films of the fight at the reservoir. They should have gone in kicking. Instead, they lost most of their people. I can't take any more orders. I must be free to run."

"I don't accept that."

Mack stopped his ministrations and looked at his brother. "I know you don't," he said softly.

"Mack," Johnny said. "What happened back there in Tel Aviv...it was all our fault."

"Was it? We didn't raise Abba and his kind on vicious hatred. We didn't put the guns in their hands. They'd be doing this whether we were here or not."

Johnny got up and went to the door. A tray of food sat in the hall. He brought it in and closed the door. "I've lost my belly for this kind of war," he said at last. "I can't do it anymore."

Mack nodded. "I understand," he said, and meant it. "We have to live our own lives as we see fit. I respect your decision. In fact, I'm pleased."

"I-I'm sorry, Mack."

"Yeah, kid," the Executioner said. "Me, too."

"You've got to promise me two things," he said. "First, don't blow what little security we have here by revealing where you are. Second, no one is to know what's happening tonight. Let me handle it. Abba's people are the only group left alive out there. I can take care of them."

Johnny stared at him for a moment. "Okay," he said finally. "You have my word."

"I guess that's it, then," Bolan said.

"Yeah, I guess so."

The Executioner finished his medical work in silence, his mind turning as much as possible to the job at hand. But one little crack had been opened, one small fissure in his rock-solid control.

He was alone.

Again.

20

Israelis all have a sense of history, of place. It is absolutely necessary to their survival as a people. This was no more evident to Mack Bolan than when he made the drive along Highway 40 to the interior city of Jerusalem.

The rolling hills of the Holy Land were dotted everywhere with the hulks of dead army vehicles that had been spray-painted and left as monuments for a culture that had to fight every day of its life simply to exist.

During the 1948 war, Jerusalem was blocked to Jews, the roads connecting the city with the rest of Israel sealed off so the people of Israel could not reach their holy place.

After some fighting in 1949, the Jews held the New City sector of Jerusalem. When the Egyptians and Syrians massed in 1967 to completely destroy the small country, the Israelis struck back hard, driving off the attackers, winning the war in just six days. Their bonus was the Old City. They retook it, David's city, *their* city. The military vehicles were a remnant of that campaign, a reminder of just how tenuous is their hold on all that is dear to them.

A reminder to be vigilant. A reminder that sometimes one has to fight. The Jews are the only surviving culture from antiquity. They survived for eighteen hundred years living nonviolently, but for eighteen hundred years they were a people without a country. Not until the Warsaw Ghetto did Jews pick up arms and fight, not until after Hitler's Holocaust and the death of six million did the Jews say, "No more."

And after that, they were unstoppable. The British held Palestine as a mandate and put immigrating Jews into camps on Cyprus. But, unstoppable, they came. They came the same way Mack and Johnny Bolan had come, by sea, in small boats. They came for the Wailing Wall and to occupy the land that had been theirs as long as memory existed.

And when the world realized that they wouldn't go away quietly, the world gave in. The United Nations partitioned the land into two countries, Israel and Jordan—Israel a Jewish state, Jordan an Arab state.

Israel is surrounded on all sides by hostile nations who want it dead. Those were the kind of odds Mack Bolan could appreciate.

Bolan drove slowly, leisurely. He had plenty of time before sunset, before his preordained confrontation with Abba.

Ever since he had stood in the church watching the wedding ceremony of Tomasso Metrano's daughter, he had wondered about the reasons for his own existence.

He knew he no longer had a life of his own. There was certainly no pleasure in the way he lived. He thrilled to the battle, but probably because it was the closest thing to emotion he was capable of. He took no joy from the killing, he knew that. Life, all life, was still precious to him—except for the life of the vermin he exterminated.

Was he like them, the ones he hunted? He searched his soul, but could find no answers. He had tried to break the cycle of death before, but the attempt had ended in failure at Stony Man Farm with the death of the woman he loved. April Rose was gone, sure, but she still lived vividly in his memory.

He had thrown himself into his missions with increasing ardor since, always pushing the odds.

Now Johnny had decided to go his own way, rejecting Bolan's crusade. He had given again, had dragged his heart out of its hiding place to be torn apart again. He didn't know if he could stand it this time.

"Damn."

An army patrol had blockaded the road a quarter mile ahead and was checking each car as it went through. He got behind a line of twenty or so cars and waited his turn.

He looked around him; extremely rocky terrain surrounded the road on all sides for about twenty yards, then climbed to sheer cliffs one hundred feet high.

Other cars were already beginning to get in line behind him. He could try to turn around and go back the way he had come, but it wouldn't leave him in any better shape. He'd still have to go through a checkpoint somewhere.

He looked at the car. Its interior was bloodstained and smelled acrid. The duffel lay on the front floor, filled with machinery of war. He was in worse shape. His face was cut and bruised, still swollen more than any makeup could help. He had no papers. There was no possible way he could bluff his way through the roadblock.

Another car eased through, then another, bringing him closer to the inevitable. His mind raced, and kept coming back to the same point: suppose he just gave up? Suppose he simply breathed out, raised his hands and let them take him? The solitude of that, the peace of it, appealed to him. He was tired and emotionally worn down.

The loss of Johnny had been a paralyzing blow to him. God damn, he deserved a life as much as anybody—the impossibility of having one was nearly maddening. He was glad his brother had had the sense to chuck this struggle. But now Bolan was alone again. Johnny and April—their faces whirled through his mind. Had he gone too far? Had he crossed the line separating humanity and the animals, the Metranos, of this world?

He was one car away from the checkpoint. Already several of the soldiers were squinting, trying to get a look into his car from a distance.

He couldn't fight it out; he was on their side. The trouble was, they didn't know that. The car in front was waved on through the roadblock, and a sergeant was motioning him up to the line.

He put the Fiat in gear and eased up to the blockade. It consisted of three armored carriers, two straddling the roadway, another pulled off on the shoulder. Several yards beyond that, an American jeep with a 50-caliber machine gun mounted on the back was parked directly in the center of the road. When someone was passed, a soldier would reverse the truck off the road and let them through. Then he'd pull it back.

Ten soldiers stood around smoking cigarettes and talking, and until the sergeant actually walked up to the window and motioned it down, Bolan had no idea of what he was going to do.

He rolled the window a third of the way down. He had never given up, ever. If this was to be his end, he'd go out like the fighter he was. He'd get it up for one more fight. Whatever will drove him, whatever war god, he would call on it again.

The sergeant spoke to him in Hebrew.

"American," he replied. "I don't understand."

"Your passport," the man said in English. "I'll need your papers."

"Sure," Bolan said, and began fumbling around in his pockets. "Here somewhere."

"You will hurry, please."

"Yeah, yeah, just a minute."

The man was reaching partway through the window, fingers wiggling impatiently—just as Bolan had hoped. He suddenly cranked the window, rolling the man's arm up tight.

Without thought, he pushed open the door, knocking the man against the hood of the car. He grabbed his duffel and ran.

He had reached the trucks before anyone could react. He jumped to the hood of one and was staring at the astonished face of the young warrior within. A second later he was over the truck, the sounds of running and shouting behind him.

He was ten feet from the jeep, its driver turning to level an Uzi at him. He heaved the duffel at the man's head, forcing him to duck, then covered the last few feet on a dead run, going up the back of the open jeep to jump on the driver.

With no time to fight, he slammed the palms of his hands on the man's ears, immediate disorientation slackening the man's face as he tumbled from the driver's seat.

The Executioner turned to the machine gun. Gunfire was rumbling as he snapped the bolt and raked the carriers, driving resistance to the ground. Then he went for tires, disabling all three vehicles with one long burst, brass casings tinkling onto the cement roadway.

As the carriers sagged like dying animals, Bolan jumped into the driver's seat and started the jeep. He took off in a hail of gunfire, his windows shattering, then the seat beside him. But within thirty seconds he had distanced himself.

This wouldn't go for long. He opened up the jeep, but didn't get much out of it. Within a couple of miles he caught up to a Toyota carrying a family.

He overtook them. When he got around a curve, he skidded to a halt, then turned to block the roadway.

The Toyota made the curve. The driver slammed on his brakes to avoid hitting the jeep. Bolan stood in the rear, manning the machine gun.

"Get out of the car!" he ordered.

The people within, two adults and three children, looked horrified, the man turning his head from side to side. The Executioner couldn't give them time to think.

He fired beside the car, the roadway churning in flying chunks of cement. "Get out of the car!"

They got out quickly, hands in the air. Bolan hated himself for scaring them, but determination kept him going. "Get off the road," he said. "Run, quickly!"

They ran.

He jumped from the jeep and hurried to the Toyota. It was still running and had a full tank of gas. He climbed in and took off.

Several miles later, he passed a convoy of army trucks, all looking for a maniac in a jeep. They passed him without a second look. Several miles after that, he saw settlements, villages carved from stone, built right into the hillsides. And beyond that, a large city sat gleaming in the hot afternoon sun.

Instinctively, he knew it was Jerusalem.

21

Johnny Bolan sat at the bar, running an index finger around the rim of the shot glass. Braxis, standing on the other side, poured himself another whiskey, leaving the half-empty bottle on the polished wood bar top. Though it was late afternoon, the room was dark, shades pulled down, no lights on.

"This stuff tastes like motor oil," Johnny said.

Braxis grunted. "Don't know," he replied. "I never drank motor oil. More?"

Johnny nodded, and Braxis refilled the small glass.

Johnny raised the drink. "To death," he said.

Braxis shrugged. "Why not?" he said. "To death."

They drank.

"You and your brother know a lot about death," Braxis said as he set his glass back on the bar.

"No," Johnny said, motioning for a refill. "Mack's the one who knows about death. I'm just a talented amateur."

"You kill for a living?"

"I never thought of it that way before," Johnny replied, "but I guess we do."

The swarthy man shook his head. "I prefer the bar."

Johnny watched as Braxis poured him another drink. "Yeah," he said. "I think I do, too."

They froze as they heard voices coming from the alley. Braxis put a finger to his lips, and the two of them sat there like hiding children as several men tried the door, shouting and banging on it when they discovered it locked.

"What if they don't go away?" Johnny whispered.

Braxis smiled knowingly. "There are other bars," he said softly. "They will not keep their money long."

A moment later, hurling last-minute curses, the men wandered off, their muffled voices drifting farther away and finally vanishing into the afternoon.

"I feel stupid sitting here like this," Johnny said.

"You don't go to kill with the big man?"

"Not this time."

Braxis brought a chuckle up from deep inside. "Maybe you don't want to die with him."

Johnny glared at the man. "What's that supposed to mean?"

Braxis returned the stare, glassy eyes shining in the semidarkness. "You are trouble, both of you," he said, and spit on the floor. "You both die, that's fine. Just die away from the house of Braxis."

"You've been well paid."

"A fool's wages," Braxis said, and spit again. "The Koran says to live in the world as one already dead. The dead are not greedy. My greed is my folly."

"The Koran says not to drink, either," Johnny said.

"So I'm a fool more than once," Braxis replied.

Johnny thought about that for a second, and his mind turned immediately to Judith. "Well, I don't intend to die either," he said. "Not by a long shot. Let's leave death to Mack Samuel Bolan."

"You are like him," Braxis said.

Johnny slammed an open palm on the bar. "No!" he said loudly. "I'm not." He couldn't sit there waiting for the obituaries anymore. "I need to use your telephone."

"No," Braxis said. "I agreed to hide you for one more day. Using the telephone is not hiding."

Johnny stood, the least bit groggy from the drinks and the pain. "For a thousand bucks a crack," he said. "I get the use of the damned phone." It was at the far end of the bar. He walked toward it, Braxis hurrying to intercept him.

"I said no." The man put his hand on the receiver.

Johnny shoved him out of the way. "Go to hell," he said, and picked up the receiver.

Angry, Braxis pulled the cord out of the wall, the unit dying in Johnny's ear.

"All right," Johnny said, letting the phone drop from his hand. "I'll use a phone somewhere else. I need some fresh air anyway." He walked to the door, unlocking it with the key in the dead bolt.

"Where are you going?" Braxis asked, his voice laced with concern.

"To start over," Johnny said, opening the door. "I'm going to start over."

He moved into the hot afternoon, Braxis slamming and locking the door behind him. He wandered the cobbled streets, sorry he had drunk so much. He wasn't falling down, but could feel he wasn't in complete control of himself either.

Trying to clear his head, Johnny walked from the alleys and into the hub of the small, stone city. The Arab population bustled all around him, carrying on their daily routines, moving through the quiet tangle of their lives, free from the burdens of responsibility that plagued him moment to moment. He envied them, envied their freedom.

He could be free, too. It wasn't too late for him. Somewhere in the world he could live like this, free from the responsibility, free from the constant vigilance, free from having to look over his shoulder. Leave vengeance to the Executioner.

He entered the main square, acrid cooking smells assaulting him. Foot and car traffic hurried in all directions. A number of cafés were set on the main drag, people sitting under colorful umbrellas at the outdoor tables, drinking Turkish coffee and talking casually.

Johnny walked to one of the small restaurants, entered the open front of the place. A man in a white apron stood squeezing oranges behind a small counter.

"Telephone?" Johnny asked.

The man reached under the counter and brought up the phone. Johnny thanked him and called Judith at Sabra headquarters. Hillel answered, and was able to get her to the phone moments later.

"Johnny?" she said, excitement lacing her voice. "You're all right!"

"I could say the same to you," he said. "I saw the films at the reservoir...."

"Please," she said. "Not over an open line. Where are you?"

"Close by," he said, thinking about the promise he had made to Mack.

"This is no time for secrecy between us," she said. "I must see you."

Johnny thought quickly. Having Judith come to Acco was certainly not the same thing as bringing her to their hiding place. He had to see her, too, to hold her, to know she was really all right.

"I'm in Acco," he said.

"Where?"

"A place on the square called the Omar Khayyám."

"Good," she said. "Is your brother...?"

"He's gone," Johnny said.

"Oh." There was a short pause. "Get some coffee, I'll be there within the hour."

"I miss you," he said, and the words sounded strange to him.

"I miss you, too," she answered.

He hung up the phone, knowing he had done the right thing, but somehow feeling he had betrayed a trust. He bought an orange juice and sat outside, watching the day wear on, feeling more comfortable, safer, with each passing minute. He didn't think about Mack and what he was doing. He thought about Judith, used Judith to push out Mack. He sobered up slowly, listening to the conversations all around him that he didn't understand, and all at once... she was there.

She stood before him, the sun behind her head, her hair glowing like a halo. She wore a soft knit dress that highlighted her figure. He had never seen her in anything but combat fatigues.

"You look beautiful," he said.

She smiled, sitting down beside him, leaning over familiarly to kiss him deeply on the mouth. He put his arms around her and hugged her fiercely to him.

"I want to be alone with you," she said into his ear.

He pulled away and looked at her. She was this far, what difference the few hundred yards to Braxis's place? Besides, Mack was wrong, paranoid. Johnny had sat there with his orange juice for a long time, everything safe, everything ordinary. Judith was the woman he loved, and he would take her to his place. It was natural. It was the thing to do.

He stood up, taking her hand. "Let's go," he said.

Arm in arm, they walked the ancient streets, women singing from the open windows, dumping out buckets of dirty dishwater to splash the stone streets near them.

"What is your brother doing now?" she asked, as they turned down the alley to Braxis's place.

"He's gone.... What difference does it make?"

"This is my country, Johnny. If he knows anything I should know..."

"As usual," Johnny said, "the Executioner is handling things himself. Here we are."

He knocked on the door. "Braxis," he said in a quiet voice. "It's me. Open up."

The door opened, the Arab's eyes widening when he saw Judith. "You're insane," he said.

"Let us in," Johnny said. "C'mon, it's okay."

Braxis opened the door, frowning, and let them pass. He stuck his head out and looked up and down the alley before closing and locking the door.

ABU'DIN QUICKLY JUMPED BACK into the shadows near the dumpster when Braxis poked his head out into the alley. He waited a moment after the man closed the door before coming out of hiding and moving back into traffic.

He hadn't seen the big man since the night he had first come to Acco, the night he had been humiliated by the man in the bar. But he had seen the pictures on the television sets and knew it was the same person.

Though he hadn't seen the big man since, this other man had been with him and, if he was still at Braxis's, could the big man be far behind?

He hurried to Majil's market, moving immediately to the phone his brother-in-law kept in his office.

They'd all see soon enough that they had humiliated the wrong person.

He dug into his wallet for the old, faded number, dialed it up. It was answered almost immediately.

"Faysal," he said. "This is Abu'din."

"Oh, hello, cousin," the voice answered suspiciously. "If you are calling about a loan..."

"No, no," Abu'din said. "I call to do *you* a favor. Do you still have those...connections you used to talk about?"

"Perhaps. What do you need?"

"I have some information for them that they might find most interesting."

"What sort of information?"

"I know where the American is. The one they call Bo-lan."

22

Sundown was approaching when Bolan pulled the Toyota into the alley behind a small tailor shop. He had driven around since entering Jerusalem two hours earlier, feeling safer in the moving vehicle, giving himself time to plan. He had been around this shop several times already, waiting for it to close. Sundown marked the beginning of Shabbat, the Jewish holy day. No work went on beyond sundown, so Bolan had only to wait.

His grim work knew no holiday.

He climbed out of the car, the last of the sun gleaming off the lofty walls of the Old City, David's city, two miles away on the high ground. Old Jerusalem was a fortress, totally surrounded by defensible walls, parts of it dating back more than two thousand years. Within those walls lived four factions: Jew, Christian, Arab and Armenian—each with its own quarter.

The Western Wall separated the Jewish and Arab quarters; an Arab holy site, the Dome of the Rock, now occupied the land where Solomon's temple once stood. It was there that Bolan was ultimately bound, there that he would take the measure of his own life, his own death amid a clash of cultures millennia old.

He looked up and down the alley, long shadows beginning to sheathe the backs of shops and houses. A young girl of about six was moving quickly toward him, a bouquet of flowers in her hand.

He stood, waiting for her to pass, but instead she ran right up to him, a large smile on her beautiful, smooth face. He returned the smile, the effort hurting him, his face still very tender.

"Shabbat shalom," she said, handing him a long-stemmed carnation from her bunch.

He took the offered gift, its touch barely felt in his callused, scarred hand. *"Shabbat shalom,"* he repeated, and was surprised to find his eyes misting.

The girl waved, then ran off, disappearing into the shadows at the end of the street.

Bolan retrieved the duffel from the interior of the Toyota and moved to the back of the tailor shop. He used one of his picks to get through the old, wooden door.

The shop was musty and very small, but for the Executioner it would serve an important purpose. He noticed that it made clothes for Hasidim, rabbinical Jews who dressed alike in black clothes. The style was centuries old, and for the Executioner, the long black coat and hat was the perfect disguise for him and his weaponry.

He quickly stripped off his street clothes and put on his blacksuit. Then he opened his makeup kit and went to work on his face.

Hasidic Jews don't shave or cut their hair in a circle around their face, so Bolan applied a black beard and improvised a hair curl on each side of his face. Then he went to the racks of clothing, finding a white shirt and black trousers to put on over his skinsuit. He left on his black jungle boots.

He picked out a black hat, then found a long overcoat, a size too big. He put on his combat harness, fitting the Linda into the shoulder holster, its extra-long clip nearly sticking out too far. The Ingram strapped neatly to his other shoulder and hung down under his arm. Over this he put the overcoat, which neatly hid everything.

In one pocket of the overcoat he put extra clips of ammo, in the other, a short-barrel .38. He was ready. Since Hasidim rarely engaged in conversation except among themselves, Bolan was set up perfectly to get around undetected and stay that way.

He rummaged in his bag and pulled out a handful of money, leaving enough to cover the cost of the outfit he was taking. Through the store's front window, beyond clothing frames and bolts of material, he could see darkness descending in earnest. It was time to go.

As he turned to leave, he saw the carnation lying atop a sewing-machine table, a gift of love in an atmosphere of hate. He picked up the flower and fixed it into his top buttonhole as a boutonniere.

TOMASSO METRANO stood watching out the window as one of Jamil's people raped a woman in the breezeway between his building and the one next to it. He didn't much like the way Jamil Arman did business, in fact he was sick to death of it. The man had no sense of honor, or of family. He was simply devious and bloodthirsty.

Metrano dropped the curtain and moved away from the window to sit on the bed. Arman was like a spider, always spinning, turning the web in on itself. Every step he took, every breath, was a way of drawing his victim up tighter in his webs. He had already gotten Big Tommy so far in over his head it would take an act of God to get him out.

Arman had Big Tommy's son, Tony, in Jerusalem, involving him more deeply in this insane jihad. Arman had gotten him, a Family head, to drop into the midst of a political maelstrom of global proportions, and then had gotten him *photographed* for the world to see.

Well, Big Tommy Metrano didn't like spiders very much. In fact he hated them. He didn't like being played for the fool, either. But all that was business, and could be forgotten if not forgiven. But the loss of his sons was deep and profound, and Guido's death he blamed directly on Arman and his webs. The loss of his sons had to be repaid in blood, first Bolan's, then Arman's. He figured on Abba for dessert.

He reached under the bed and slid out his suitcase. He pulled it up on the bed, dumped out the clothes and lifted the false bottom. Beneath, his matching pearl-handled .45s sat gleaming in their contoured case.

He'd bide his time until Tony came back, probably until the party. He wondered about the party, for by now he was sure that there was no ten million bucks coming into his hands. It was a set-up. Arman probably intended to use blackmail to keep Metrano in line, keep him supplying guns without benefit of payment. Perhaps he'd threaten to expose his "connections" with the ganglord.

It didn't matter, really. He just didn't take that kind of crap. He'd have to fight his way out, of course, but he'd fought his way out of tough spots before.

He lifted one of the guns out of the case and turned it around in his hands. He'd take out Arman himself. It had been quite a while since he'd dropped the hammer on anybody personally. He was going to enjoy it.

ABBA WATCHED LAZILY out the tinted back seat window of the Mercedes as it pulled up near the main gates of Acco, the car's air-conditioning doing very little to keep out the late-afternoon heat.

"There he is," the driver said, pointing to a man frantically waving to them just outside the gates.

"Pull over," Abba said, and stole a glance at the other two men sitting in the car with him. They looked anxious, yes, and hungry. They would work quite nicely for him.

They pulled off the road, the Arab hurrying over to meet them. Abba rolled down his window and motioned the man over. "You are the man who called us?"

"Yes," Abu'din said, nodding. "Bo-lan came here two nights ago, in the middle of the night. When I asked him questions, he attacked me. A vicious pig. Vicious."

"Yes, yes," Abba said, impatient. He didn't have much time here. He needed to get back to Jerusalem before sunset. "Is Bolan in there now?"

"I don't know," the Arab said. "The one who travels with him is, though. He is there with a woman."

Abba brightened. "A woman?"

"A Jew, I think. Maybe military."

Abba cracked the door. "You will get in and take us to this place."

"No!" Abu'din said, backing away. "I'm not looking for any trouble." He held up a piece of paper. "Here. I have drawn you a map."

"Bring it here," Abba said.

The man moved tentatively toward the car, the paper outstretched in his hand. Abba took it from him and handed it to the driver. "Can you find this place?"

The driver grunted affirmatively.

"Good," Abba said cheerily and held up a stack of bills. "Your reward."

Abu'din moved up to the car, Abba pulling back the bills until Abu'din was reaching far into the car for them.

"Try this instead," Abba said, pointing the MR 73 at the Arab's face.

Abu'din's eyes went wide, and Abba jammed the long barrel into his mouth until he gagged.

"Now I want you to close your mouth around it tight," Abba said.

Abu'din was shaking wildly. He closed his mouth on the barrel, the question loud in his eyes.

Abba decided to answer him. "I wanted to muffle the report," he said, and pulled the trigger, the back of the man's head splattering off with a smoky pop, his body dropping into the tall grass immediately.

"Let us go," Abba said. "We do not have much time."

23

Johnny Bolan closed and locked the door, turning to stare at Judith, who was in turn staring at him. Emotions collided within him, his feelings a jumble. The one thing he did know, however, was that he wanted to be with this woman, to be with her as long as she wanted him to.

"I never thought it would happen this way," she said.

"What way?" he asked, and moved toward her. Now that he had her here alone in his room, he felt awkward, unsure of himself. But she melted into his arms and all the fears vanished immediately.

"You," she said. "Us. In the middle of all this, with death our companion, I choose to fall in love... with an American killer, no less."

He pulled away from her. "I'm no killer," he said.

She smiled at him, touched the bruises on his face with gentle fingers. "No, you're not. What happened to you?"

He told her about Tel Aviv, leaving out nothing. When he was through, she sat on his bed, her face strained in concentration. "Then many of them are still out there," she said.

He nodded. "Yes."

She frowned. "I was afraid of that. Where is your brother now?"

He turned away from her. "My brother follows his own path. Let's not think of him anymore."

She stood and walked to Johnny, hugging him from behind. "We must think of him," she said into his shoulder. "His shadow hangs over everything we do."

He turned to her then, took her shoulders in his hands. "He's the Executioner," he said. "And he's out plying his trade."

"That's easy enough to say," she replied. "It's not your land, your people coming under the gun."

"You're my people," he said. "And your country is mine, too. I'm not trying to be callous, but I've decided to try and escape the hold he has on me."

"Just tell me where he is. My people can back him."

"You don't get it," he said. "While you were losing your lives at the reservoir, he was taking care of just as many all by himself. He doesn't need you."

"Suppose he fails?"

Johnny moved away from her and stretched out on the bed, staring at the ceiling. "I can't answer that."

She moved to sit beside him, laying her head on his chest. "Just tell me where he is."

"I—I can't. I've already broken one promise by bringing you up here. I won't break another. Please don't ask me to."

She sat up and looked deeply into his eyes. "All right," she answered quietly, her smile a sad one. "For you I put my fears away because I trust you. Am I wrong to do that, Johnny Bolan?"

"No," he answered hoarsely. "I'll always be here to calm your fears."

She stood, her eyes locking softly with his, her features a portrait of vulnerability. Reaching behind her, she undid the zipper in the back of her dress, letting the garment drop to the floor. Bra and panties followed, and she stood naked before him.

He reached out for her, pulling her onto the bed with him. Johnny's heart was pounding, his breathing ragged. She was so childlike, so yielding, that when he folded her into his arms, he wanted the gesture to be as much protective as it was sexual.

They lay wrapped up that way for a long time until their mutual need drove them toward fulfillment. And when the moment came for both of them, Johnny felt an exhilaration, the hope of a new and better life washing over him like high tide.

Afterward, they clung to each other, and Johnny experienced a kind of fullness that he remembered from his earliest childhood. He was going back, recapturing an emotional world that he had forgotten even existed.

Outside, the sky was beginning to darken.

"Almost Shabbat," Judith said, and kissed him lightly on the lips. "I wish you *shabbat shalom*."

"What does that mean?"

She smiled. "Shabbat is a time of great celebration in Israel. It is the day we give to God and to the pleasures he has given us. It is the day of the week when we put everything else aside and remember what it means to be human."

He smiled. *"Shabbat shalom,"* he repeated, and drew her close. "Every day will be like Shabbat for us."

"Yes," she said. "That would truly be a wonderful thing...but..." Judith sat up, reaching for her clothes.

"What are you doing?" he asked.

"I promised Hillel I'd check in before sunset," she said. "Just a call . . . I'll be right back."

"No, wait," he said, afraid that Hillel would think of some reason why she should go to Haifa. "Why don't you stay here and take it easy, and I'll go phone for you."

He pushed her back gently. "You'll spoil me," she said.

"Oh, yes."

He had to cross over her to get to his own clothes, the feel of her body exciting him again. She shyly covered herself with her arms. "Not now, after you've done what you were supposed to do."

"Okay."

She winked playfully. "Tell Hillel that I might not make it back to headquarters tonight."

He stood and began dressing quickly. "I'll definitely tell Hillel you won't make it back tonight."

He finished dressing and hurried out the door, taking the stairs two at a time. The bar was quiet, and nearly pitch-dark. Braxis wasn't in the bar, but Johnny could hear his television playing in an adjoining room.

The phone sat on the end of the bar. He hurried to it, forgetting that Braxis had pulled it out of the wall. He picked it up to find it dead.

"Damn."

Disappointed, he let the receiver fall to the bar top and ran to the door. He'd go to the café and call from there. He'd be back in fifteen minutes.

He unlocked the door and hurried into the alley, jogging the distance to the coffee shop along the ever-darkening streets.

The call to Hillel went uneventfully. He told the man that all was quiet and hopefully would stay that way, and Hillel passed a message back that the remaining ten Sabra agents in country were at the *mikva* and would remain for the evening.

The smells of evening meals cooking filled the ocean-cooled twilight air. He strolled back casually, filled with a sense of belonging, of fulfillment. Perhaps the dark night had passed. Perhaps the constant swimming against the tide could finally ease. He had done his part. He had soldiered with the best of them—the Executioner. Now, on Shabbat he was going to become a civilian again. He was going to put the fighting and the killing behind him and rejoin the human race. How did Judith put it? He was going to remember what it meant to be a human being.

The wailing came up softly, like the call of a distant bird. His mind ignored it at first, pushing it to a far, unused corner. But soon he couldn't resist the sounds as they drew closer.

A group of Arabs was coming across the square from the front gate. Several of the women were wailing and crying. They carried something with them, on their shoulders.

As the townspeople hurried to the entourage, Johnny felt himself moving with them. He knew what he'd find before he got there.

The group carried a body on an old wooden door, its head simply an empty cavity. The face, unfortunately, he recognized. It was the man his brother had fought the first night in Acco.

"No," he whispered low. Then louder, a plea, "No!"

He turned and bolted, his mind a totally separate thing from his body as he watched himself from outside, running back to Braxis's tavern. He kept picturing himself finding Judith naked and laughing, kissing away his fears, drawing him into herself. But the vision was hazy, ill-defined, and the panic he felt couldn't be reasoned away.

He reached the tavern in minutes. The front door stood open. He rushed in without a thought for himself, and nearly tripped over the body of Braxis.

The man lay on the floor, chairs and tables overturned all around him, a record of the last seconds of his life. His body lay torn open from close-range SMG fire, organs exposed, incredible amounts of blood splattered everywhere.

Johnny took all of this in in an instant, his legs carrying him toward the stairs and Judith. He had vaulted several steps before the fighter's instinct took hold.

A sixth sense made him jump to the side, just as a man stood up from behind the bar firing an M-16.

The noise rattled loudly in the small room, the banister exploding and collapsing as Johnny let himself fall backward, rolling down the stairs as another burst traced his path.

He hit the ground and dived for the bar, the gunner's vision obscured by the bar itself. When the man rounded the obstacle to finish the job, he was confronted by a charging madman, growling like a wild animal.

Johnny plowed into him on a dead run, momentum carrying them both toward the chewed-up stairs. They banged hard, the gun dropping from the man's hands as the wind went out of him.

Johnny grabbed him by the ears, bashing his head against the remnants of the banister, the man's face contorting in agony. Then Johnny grabbed the terrorist's lapels and threw him back toward the bar.

The man slammed into it and fell to the floor, nearly unconscious. Johnny dived on him after grabbing the whiskey bottle that he and Braxis had shared earlier.

The man's eyes cleared somewhat, just in time to see Johnny break the bottle on the side of the bar and raise his arm. He tried to scream, but his voice was cut off as Johnny Bolan buried half a broken bottle in his face.

Johnny was up, taking the M-16 as an afterthought. He pounded up the stairs, the door to his room hanging open also. He knew what he would find before he got there, but the horror of it still drove him to his knees.

Judith lay, still naked, on the floor. Blood was pooled all around her legs, her dead eyes opened wide in pain and terror.

She had obviously been raped. On her stomach, a six-pointed Star of David had been carved with a knife.

Johnny crawled to her, kissing her still-warm lips and closing her eyes. "My love," he whispered.

Then he saw the note. It lay on the floor next to her head. It read: Sorry you missed the party, but your girlfriend showed us a good time anyway. See you in Jerusalem. Abba.

The note was written in blood—Judith's blood.

Johnny stood slowly. He moved to the bed like a zombie and took the spread from it. Abba. Here. Mack had told him this would happen, had warned him the only way he knew how.

He walked to Judith, took one last look at her face, then covered her.

"*Shabbat shalom,*" he whispered, then he turned his head and threw up.

After his stomach was as empty as his soul, he stood and moved back to the bed. Underneath it were the weapons they still had left. He placed them on the bed, then pulled the ends of the sheet together to bundle them.

Now he understood.

24

The Executioner left the Toyota on Mamilla Street with the key under the front seat. He climbed the long hill toward the Old City. Vacant dilapidated buildings surrounded him. Darkness was descending quickly now, nature's props for the carnage to come.

All of Israel was still reeling from the events of the past two days; a large crowd was flowing toward David's city to pray at the wall. If the PLO had its way, when the wall went up, a great many people would go up with it.

The destruction of the Western Wall would be a huge effort. The *HaKotel*, as it is called, stands one hundred feet high and faces a massive courtyard. It is built of solid rock two feet thick. Whatever Abba and his henchmen had in mind would be nasty.

Mamilla joined Hativat Yerushalayim at the Jaffa Gate. Bolan, dressed in the meekest of costumes, crossed over and entered the gate with the Shabbat crowds. He passed David's Citadel, and entered a world forgotten by time.

The Israelites had built this city thousands of years before, but others had known it, too. The Muslims under Saladin had held it, and the Turks, as well as European Crusaders and British on a different crusade.

The Romans had razed it in 70 A.D., only to rebuild it and lose it themselves. It is a city lost to time and place, and within its several-mile area are contained the most important relics of the three greatest religions on the planet.

Along with the Western Wall, Muhammad's rock stands several hundred yards away from the trail Jesus took to Calvary, the place of his crucifixion on which a church is now built. The history of many peoples resides within David's city, histories that Bolan felt pressing against him here at the crossroads of Planet Earth.

Bolan felt himself overwhelmed, dwarfed by the magnitude of what confronted him. He realized that his own feelings, his own internal conflicts, meant nothing compared to the immensity of the task that confronted him. He dared to call on Jerusalem to be the arbiter of his destiny. His own arrogance astounded him.

He moved straight ahead, picking the first street in a maze of arteries. He was in the Muslim quarter, a place called David's Street by the Israelis, and Chain Street by the inhabitants. Jerusalem is built on hills, the streets merely a series of steps wide enough for two people to pass side by side.

Not a good place to fight a war.

Bolan moved into the crowd at a pace that would appear pious. The steps of the street were jammed with people. On either side, small stalls filled every inch, their Arab owners selling spicy foods, clothes and handmade items, business as usual for two thousand years. The smell of burning hashish assaulted him from every third or fourth stall.

In a matter of minutes he was totally closed in. Narrow and winding, the street swallowed him up as if the entire universe existed on its narrow byway. People shoved, as young boys yelling, "'Cuse, 'cuse, 'cuse," moved through the lines of people carrying trays of *bag-el*, local bread, above their heads. Dark wrinkled faces of old men peered inscrutably at the moving crowd from the depths of the stalls. And it was then, just then, that Bolan knew his test would come soon. He beseeched the universe to spare the innocents on the streets.

FAISEL IBN FAISEL SAT on the high stool, the snaking stem of the hookah set comfortably between his lips, bittersweet hash smoke rising indolently from the bowl of the tall, ornately carved pipe.

He watched.

Tourists and faithful moved past his vantage point in the wood-carving shop, and sometimes he felt as if the entire world would one day walk past this place. But the entire world did not interest Faisel ibn Faisel—it was only one man he sought.

He remembered the old days before 1967, when the Jews weren't allowed to visit their accursed Wall, or come to Muhammad's city at all. Perhaps, after tonight, they would come no longer. And it was one man, they said, one man who stood between his nephew, Abba, and the destruction of the Wall—the man they called the Executioner.

The walkie-talkie squawked loudly beside him. He picked it up and pushed in the button. *"Salaam,"* he said loudly into the instrument.

"Wa alaikum as salaam," came the distorted reply. "We have seen no one come through here yet."

"I have seen no one either."

"Perhaps the American does not come."

"Yes, I... Wait a moment." Faisel ibn Faisel squinted into the crowd on Chain Street. Among those moving in the direction of the Jewish quarter was a Hasid.

He had seen many of them come through here since '67, in their black outfits and coats, but none, not one, had ever worn a flower in his lapel. They were always plain, always the same. He pushed the button back in and spoke in a whisper. "The devil is passing me now. He is dressed as a Jew, a Hasidic rabbi. He is large, huge, and wears a flower on his coat lapel. Pass the word."

Faisel turned off the radio and reached under his *mishla*, his hand closing around the butt of the Colt Python that rested there. He drew out the 357 Magnum and flipped out the cylinder to check the .38

Special load. The American was big, but he was human. All the precautions seemed trivial at this point. He would finish the big man himself—right now.

He pushed the hookah aside and stepped into the street.

BOLAN, SENSES HONED, moved carefully, his head turning just slightly, his eyes continually shifting from side to side. He caught a flash of peripheral movement behind him, saw a glint of metal in the old man's hand and had a second to wonder at such sloppiness before swinging around, the Linda filling his hand.

"Down!" he yelled as he pivoted. The crowd screamed and dived for cover, leaving on their feet only an old man with a Colt Magnum and his executioner.

The Arab was no fighter. Bolan's action froze him, his face wide-eyed. They stood postured for several beats, facing death across a human sea, the realization of his own end filling the Arab's face. Then reality flooded in, other voices, other guns—everywhere.

The Arab tried to fire, but Bolan's single shot caught him chest-high before the oldtimer could even pull the trigger. He fell back into the stall, brass and carved wood clattering everywhere as a woman shrieked loudly.

The Executioner turned to see rifles poking out of stalls on both sides of the steps. Presents from Abba. He raked a burst at full auto across the stalls, then jumped into the closest one for protection.

Civilians were up, trying to scramble away as the Arabs opened up with SMGs, the noise rumbling in the streets as people fell bleeding to the stone steps.

Bolan slid to the ground, the thin, wooden sides of the stall ripping apart in long splinters as earrings and knickknacks danced and fell under the hail of lead.

A woman and child were huddled in the back of the shop. Bolan motioned them down, then turned streetside, firing at two gunners who charged down the stairs from the other direction.

The first was an obese, bearded man with an old Lee-Enfield rifle. Bolan ripped his belly open on auto, guts spewing from the gaping wound. The man's momentum carried him farther down the stairs, blood gushing from his mouth and nose until he tumbled over the body of a tourist and fell into a vendor's cart, ice cream tumbling all over the steps. The second hitter tried to duck into a stall, but Bolan emptied the clip as he led him in, the man falling out of the stall seconds later, half of his face blown away.

Bolan retreated and unstrapped the Ingram, taking a second to jam another clip in the Linda. He jumped back out again, using the overturned ice-cream cart for cover. He opened up the Ingram as the world came apart around him, bullets pinging off the metal ice-box of the cart and thudding into the bodies already littering the steps.

He heard crashing from inside a stall as a man fell, dead there. Another came partway out, firing wildly with an M-16, muzzle-flash lighting the darkening street. Bolan held a beat, letting him exhaust the clip, then jumped, stitching the man up his left side as he turned to duck into the shop.

The sound of firing erupted behind the Executioner, and he dived back across the steps and into his stall as more men with guns charged down the steps. A sandwich, with Bolan as the meat.

He grabbed the expended clip from the MAC-10 and threw it aside, jamming another into place. He came around the opening, dicing another terrorist coming down for him, while the others took up positions inside the stall. Turning quickly, he fired a burst farther down the stairs, then fell back in.

The sound came up behind him faster than he could react. He turned in time to see a heavy vase arcing toward his head in the hands of the woman he had protected in the stall.

It smashed on his head, bringing darkness spotted with brown. He fought unconsciousness with the will of a demon, standing to throw the woman out onto the steps and the fate that awaited anyone who stepped out there. But he fell behind her, control of his motor functions gone, and rolled down the stairs.

Then hands were all over him, beating him—killing him.

25

He barely felt the punches, the kicks. Stunned from the blow to the head, he resisted feebly the army of silhouettes that pounded him, grunting and laughing gutturally in the darkness of Chain Street. His mind was whirring, the life instinct struggling to take hold, to propel him away from the certain death that was slowly overtaking him.

He took a foot to the side of the face, his vision blurring, the false beard ripping from his chin. He clung desperately to consciousness, wanting to be awake for the end. Then, through the dark prison of legs that surrounded him, he saw it.

One of the bodies that littered the steps was struggling to rise. One of the wounded, a woman, got weakly to her knees. Then, using his discarded MAC-10 as a crutch, she made it to her feet.

She stood, weaving, observed by no one except Bolan, the others too intent on punishing him. She raised the Ingram with familiarity, all Israelis being schooled in the use of firearms, and braced it against the crook of her arm.

She jammed the trigger, firing point-blank on full auto into the crowd of thugs, bright flashes flaring the night.

They fell away, screaming, blood spattering everywhere, raining down upon Bolan. She didn't stop firing until they were all down.

A big man had fallen on top of the Executioner. He wriggled out from under and faced the specter. She stood, not five feet from him, the smoking machine gun still tucked in her arm, unsure of whether to kill him or not.

There was something about her. There, in the dark, her features clouded by the night, she seemed familiar. He blinked as the woman took another faltering step toward him. Tears came to his eyes. No. This was insane.

The words wrenched from his swollen lips. "April..." he said. "April...?"

She took another step, the apparition of April Rose, her own bloody lips moving into a slow smile... and she fell to the steps, dead, the Ingram falling from her hands to slide within inches of Bolan's fingers.

He crawled to her body and cradled her head in his lap. Close now, he could see she wasn't April and couldn't have been at all. The woman's body was ripped and bloody. He couldn't imagine what had kept her alive this long. His eyes, the light, must have played tricks on him.

"Thanks," he said quietly, and smoothed her hair out of her face, closing her eyes. He laid her head gently back on the hard ground.

His head pounded. He was dizzy and disoriented. The Ingram was empty. He struggled to get the clip out and pulled another from his pocket.

He could hear voices farther up the steps, but they were swallowed in the darkness. He had to keep moving.

He stood on shaky legs, going back to the stall where he had been hit to retrieve the Linda. He heard movement on top of the stall. Turning the MAC-10 up, he traced a burst at the ceiling. Seconds later, a body fell silently from the roof, crumpling to the stairs.

He drew off the heavy coat and white shirt, sticking the extra clips and the .38 in the waistband of his pants. He still had a distance to cover before reaching the Wailing Wall. All in black now, he merged with the darkness.

The street was quiet as he stepped out onto it, but he knew they were out there, waiting. His head still spun as he continued down the steps, picking his way around the bodies.

It was a dark and twisted nightmare world of black, looming shapes and disjointed sounds. In the distance he could hear a bell tolling, the call to prayer for the Muslims. He didn't think the ones after him would bother to stop for prayers.

He looked up. Another Arab terrorist ran the rooftops ten feet overhead. He took the man out in midstride, the body falling with a loud scream to the stairs. One above on his right, ready to fire. He ran toward him, going right under him and firing upward again. Thuds on the pavement as several of them jumped down to face him.

With the Linda in one hand, the Ingram in the other, he jumped from the stall immediately, firing in both directions at the same time. The Linda churned a bearded man's chest as he fell, firing, to the ground, choking on his own blood seconds later. The Ingram had jumped away from Bolan when he fired it, cutting a jagged line straight up the other guy's torso. The man stumbled, then died on his feet, pitching head first down the stairs.

Bolan ran then. Still hurting, he forced his body to move, to react mechanically, instinctively. When he heard firing behind him, he ducked into a stall and came out shooting up the stairs, driving back the opposition, immediately charging off again.

A dark form above—he looked up to see a shadow with a long knife jumping at him. The guy hit hard, both of them falling and rolling down the stairs. Bolan managed to get a knee to the man's groin, and pulled the Linda from the shoulder holster as the man's body sagged under the blow.

They rolled into a glass case of earrings, shattering it. Bolan jammed the Linda under the guy's chin and pulled the trigger, taking his head off.

The Executioner was up again, stumbling, moving forward. Chain Street dead-ended at a wall where Bet Ha Bad crossed it. A quick jog to the right and Chain picked up again, except here it was called Ha-Shalshelet.

He came around the corner, the Ingram ready, and ran into a band of Abba's blacksuits. He was getting close. There must have been six or eight of them.

He fired, sending them searching for cover. This wasn't going to work, there were too many behind him. Then an idea came to him.

Running back, he picked up Chain again, firing at a group of Abba's henchmen thirty feet up the stairs. He then jogged around to Ha-Shalshelet, firing sporadically, doing no more than drawing them to him like rabbits to headlights. Then he retraced his steps to Chain, repeating the procedure, drawing them forward, then diving into one of the stalls as they charged.

As Abba's blacksuits came around the dead end onto Chain, Bolan jumped out of the stall, firing in both directions, then diving back in again.

Everyone fired at once, in the dark neither band knowing the other was there. Caught in their own cross fire, the two groups tore hell out of each other, most of them dying before they knew what had happened. When the firing let up, Bolan jumped out again.

A few men still stood, confused, wounded. Bolan took out two of Abba's people, then turned and got another one on the steps.

So much for the warm-up. Now for the main event. Bolan checked his load, then charged around the cul-de-sac and headed down Ha-Shalshelet for the wall.

The street was totally deserted, shops and stalls abandoned by frightened owners. Bolan walked on deliberately, feeling the pull of his destiny. All his questions would be answered here. The dull ache that had gnawed at him since the Catholic church in West Palm Beach had turned into a full-blown pain. What was he worth?

In the distance, Ha-Shalshelet dead-ended just as Chain had. But there were no more streets after that. This dead end meant he had reached his destination. He began to hear a sound, low-pitched, almost like the howl of the wind. He couldn't place it.

He kept walking, the sound getting louder. There would undoubtedly be opposition at the Ha-Shalshelet wall entry. He drew a sound suppressor out of his combat harness and fitted it on the Linda. Silence was essential now.

He neared the dead end, the wall's courtyard a right turn away. Hugging the far right of the street, he made the crossroads. On the blank wall in front of him was a small sign written in English: Western Wall. An arrow indicated the direction. This was it.

He jumped into the opening, the Linda stiff-armed out in front of him. He peered down a narrow passageway ten feet long, and saw three men armed with SMGs at the other end.

He fired on auto, two of the men spinning quickly to the ground. The third jumped away from the opening, Bolan charging in after him.

He emerged in an open space as large as a football stadium, the sound loud, overpowering. He now realized where the noise was coming from: several thousand people stood facing the wall, moaning, wailing. The wall stood huge and imposing at the far end of the large courtyard.

The third guy was screaming across the courtyard, his cries swallowed up in the sounds of the crowd, as he tried to prime his M-16. Bolan took him out with a dead-center burst, and his body fell from the small plateau on which they stood to the mass of chanting humanity below.

Bolan passed a small guard shack, several Israeli army regulars piled up dead around it, and stared at the wall. He wasn't prepared for its size, its magnificence.

More than twenty of Abba's blacksuits were working on it, laying C-4 plastique and cases of dynamite all along its incredible length, as much destructive power as the Executioner had ever seen in one place. The crowd was held at bay by men with submachine guns, people already lying dead, many others tied up near the wall, holding explosives, some with dynamite sticks in their mouths. The moaning was their chant of sadness and loss for the wall, for their heritage.

Bolan was overwhelmed, his arms dropping slowly to his side. What kind of events had brought him to this place? Should he further desecrate it with more killing, or was he, like many of those in the courtyard, there to martyr himself? Had his years of bloodshed accomplished anything at all or was he simply another mad dog to be put to sleep? Could he have been wrong all this time? His own brother thought so.

The fight was gone from him, drained away by pain and loss. If it was time for him to die, so be it.

TONY METRANO CROUCHED in the guard shack, watching the Executioner from the cut-out window. He almost laughed, it would be so easy. The idiot was just standing there, waiting for someone to take him out.

Tony straightened quietly, bringing the M-16 slowly up to his shoulder. He fixed the man in black in his sights, then stroked the trigger lightly, lovingly.

26

Mack Bolan's combat senses sent the short hairs prickling on the back of his neck. But even as he turned, he knew it was too late. He was finished. Things seemed to move in slow motion and the Ingram weighed a ton as he tried to drag the weapon into target acquisition before Tony Metrano could blow him away.

But just short of the flash point, Metrano screamed, his hand exploding off the stock of the M-16, part of his face disintegrating under a burst of silenced MAC-10 frenzy.

The Executioner turned to see his brother staring hard, smoke still curling from the barrel of the Ingram. Behind him, the remnants of Sabra stood, looking grim, looking hard.

Bolan watched Johnny stride slowly toward him, and something about the man looked different.

He wasn't a kid anymore.

Johnny walked to within inches of Bolan, the two locking eyes; Johnny's were diamond-hard, and just as cold.

"You were right," he said.

Bolan searched those eyes. "Was I?" he asked.

Johnny slung the Ingram over his shoulder and took his brother by the arms. "About everything," he said, and the Executioner didn't need to ask any questions, for the story was right there, written in pain in Johnny's eyes.

He looked at Johnny, and thought about the fact that he had been saved twice tonight—once by a dead woman, perhaps a long-dead woman. Mack Bolan wasn't a religious man, not in the orthodox sense, but something had spared him when he walked to the chasm. And maybe he'd been spared for a reason.

Johnny had been the vehicle for his own self-doubts, and Johnny now stood before him, a mirror of himself. There *was* a difference between him and those he fought against. It was the difference between right and wrong, between human and savage—it was the difference that kept civilization and all that was good and holy one step away from the jungle.

Where Mack Bolan lived was a dark and lonely place, but it was his place, his mission.

Johnny nodded toward the Sabra agents. "Me and the others," he said, "figured to stop some cannibals here tonight. Care to join us?"

Bolan turned and watched the distant spectacle at the wall. The terrorists were hurrying to complete the laying of the charges. The wailing still droned on, rising in pitch and intensity. Abba's people still hadn't seen Bolan and Johnny there in the shadows across the courtyard, or if they did, they probably thought it was their men.

Taking Johnny to him, he hugged him fiercely. "I'm sorry," he whispered, and said a silent prayer for Judith Meyers. Then he pulled away and put a new clip in the Ingram. He stared at the Sabra agents. "No prisoners, okay?"

To a man, they nodded, Hillel most vehemently.

"Do you have a plan?" Johnny asked.

Bolan smiled grimly. "Yeah," he said. "We wade in and blow them away."

Johnny returned the smile. "We brought along something that might help."

Several of the Sabras brought out heavy tote bags, and began pulling gas masks out of them, passing them around. Then they dug out the canisters.

"Tear gas," Johnny said, handing his brother one of the masks. "Here. Put this on."

Bolan fitted the mask over his face, snugging it up with the adjustable straps. He shot Johnny the thumbs-up sign, and slung his own Ingram on his shoulder, filling his free hands with tear gas.

Ten stone steps led down to the courtyard proper. Bolan led his small, determined band of freedom fighters down the stairs. Hillel, arm still in a sling, led the Sabras.

They moved into the crowd, mourners parting with gasps as they marched through. In the rear sections, people began running up the steps as they realized they weren't being held back any longer.

Mack and Johnny strode through the crush of people shoulder to shoulder, the others fanning out to cover the length of the wall.

The terrorists were beginning to realize that something had gone wrong as they saw a stream of people escaping the enclosed courtyard. They were waving to one another, shouting. Bolan kept moving, drawing closer and closer. There was nowhere to hide down here; it was all open, flat ground. All that separated the Executioner from his quarry were fifty feet and a curtain of humanity.

But the curtain was beginning to part, the crowds shying from the commandos. Bolan elbowed Johnny and began pulling the pins from the tear gas canisters.

He lobbed the first one. It arced through the night on a streamer of bright white, bouncing against the wall to spew smoke everywhere.

One of the terrorists fired into the crowd, and all at once tear gas was coming from everywhere. The crowd scattered, charging madly in all directions, as Bolan and Johnny broke into a run.

Smoke filled the proximity of the wall, and the Executioner charged into the dense fog. He knew the wind would dissipate it soon, so they'd have to make use of the fumes' effects immediately.

He saw a muzzle-flash through the haze of smoke and fired at it; a terrorist stumbled into view and fell near his feet. Then the night was ripped apart by the rattling of submachine guns.

Civilians threw themselves to the ground, coughing and crying from the gas and utter terror. Better that, Bolan thought, than on their feet getting killed.

A terrorist ran past him. Bolan turned and blew off the man's head at six feet. The body took ten more paces before collapsing.

Hillel dashed past, his Desert Eagle in his good hand. Bolan almost shot him accidently, holding up at the last second. He smiled, the reflexes strong again.

The smoke began to roll into the night sky, visibility clearing somewhat. Bolan saw his men, up and down the wall, pounding the terrorists, ripping them to shreds with automatic fire.

The Executioner saw two Arabs rushing the wall, trying to touch off the charges. The first he got on the run, the man's back exploding, his body somersaulting forward. The second made the wall and was trying to join the electrical connection with the blasting caps when Bolan tore a hole right through him.

And as the smoke cleared, his people were mopping up. Blacksuits littered the stone courtyard. A few were on their knees, fingers scrabbling at their burning eyes. They were dispatched quickly and finally. Remarkably, none of the hostages tied to the wall was hurt.

Bolan ripped his mask off and began looking for Abba. The two thousand people remaining in the courtyard rushed to their wall, their cries now of pure happiness as they untied the hostages and pulled the explosives down and away.

Bolan and Johnny walked along the line of dead, searching for the mastermind of such sickness. Occasional shots rang out as Hillel moved to each body, putting a bullet through the head of those who still lived.

Abba was not among the dead. Rather than wait around to go down with the ship, he must have taken off, leaving his men to face death by themselves. Bolan shook his head. It figured.

"We have to get out of here," Johnny said.

Bolan nodded, looking around the courtyard. It was surrounded on all sides by walls, some of which had doors in them. "Can we get out that way?" he asked.

"The doors lead to the Arab quarter," Hillel said, walking up. "God only knows what could be waiting for us on the other side."

"Yeah," Bolan said. "Gather your people, then let's go out the way we came in."

Hillel nodded and called to the others in Hebrew, then he turned back to the Executioner. "It's the most amazing thing," he said.

"What?"

"The wall . . . it's undamaged. Not a nick, not a bullet hole. It's totally untouched."

Bolan smiled. "I guess we're better shots than we thought," he said.

The warriors gathered. They moved in a group toward the far end of the courtyard where they had come in, two thousand people breaking into spontaneous applause and cheers as they passed.

"What now?" Hillel asked as they walked.

Bolan looked at him with raised eyebrows. "You're still with me?"

"As long as you want us," one of the others said.

The Executioner nodded, knowing they were his kind of warriors. No other words were necessary. "You know," he said, "Johnny and I came here for a reason. We haven't accomplished it yet."

"Metrano," Johnny said.

"He's at the Rosh Hanikra kibbutz," Hillel said.

"I know," Bolan said.

Hillel chuckled. "He's got many hostages and several hundred soldiers with him."

"I can hardly wait," the Executioner said.

Johnny raised a clenched fist. "Me either."

Bolan looked at the others. "It won't be easy," he said. "We'll probably get ourselves killed at a party like this. Are you with me?"

They yelled affirmation. "Try and keep us away," Hillel said.

They reached the end of the courtyard and climbed the stone stairs to the guard shack. There, trying to crawl across the ground, was Tony Metrano. One hand was gone, nothing but a bloody stump. His face was only half there, one of his eyes gone completely.

"Well," said Johnny. "Look what we have here. The man who likes penknives."

Johnny bent down, his face contorted by rage. "Hurt your hand, Tony?" he said. He was about to stomp on Metrano's ruined arm, when Bolan rushed up to him.

"No!" Bolan said. He pulled Johnny away from the man.

"What the hell are you doing?" Johnny asked.

"If you do this, then you're the same as they are," Bolan said.

Bolan pulled the .38 out of his waistband. He moved to the pathetic figure and put a mercy round through his brain.

Johnny just stared at him.

"Listen to me," the Executioner told his brother. "I know how badly you hurt right now. Believe me, I know the anger, the frustration. But if we act like them, if we take pleasure from the killing... we don't deserve life either."

Johnny Bolan looked at the ground, the shame welling up in him. In that instant, he truly understood his brother completely and knew the face of real compassion.

27

Abba waited until the first tear gas canister bounced against the wall, then decided it was time to move on. He skirted the wall, gaining passage through one of the doors that led out of the courtyard and into the Arab quarter. Arab soldiers manned the door, passing him on recognition.

"Lock this," he said. "Let no one else through."

Within seconds, the fighting started in earnest. He hurried away, putting distance between himself and the battle. Abba was angry. It was all Tony Metrano's fault. If he had let Abba kill the Americans when he wanted to, none of this would have happened. Instead, the Executioner was running around loose, causing havoc.

Well, no matter. By now, Arman had probably talked the Mafia man into continuing their relationship on a regular basis. They could do this again next week, next month, whenever they wanted.

He found his white Mercedes where he had left it near Dung Gate. He climbed behind the wheel and got out of there, passing truckloads of Israeli military when he turned onto Derekh Yeriho Street, and out of the Old City.

He pointed the car east, back in the direction of Rosh Hanikra. Because of the damned American, things hadn't gone according to plan, but the campaign hadn't been entirely unsuccessful, either.

It had thrown the Jewish entity into a panic and would continue to do so.

Terrorism is the absolute, most effective means of waging war. It strikes at the very heart of a people, destroying their will by attacking without reason their most sacred institutions and their weakest numbers. Fear is the key.

Next time, Abba thought, they would concentrate totally on schools, hospitals and retirement homes—easy targets with high visibility.

But for now, they still had Rosh Hanikra and all its hostages. Even now the organization was moving more troops to the border, ready to bring in the captives. Rosh Hanikra was a toehold. With luck and proper manipulation of the hostages, it could be the beginning of the Palestinian state. And even if the Israelis were to attack the kibbutz, they would lose all their hostages, a demoralizing victory, and one that would make the citizens live in fear wherever they were.

Abba got out of Jerusalem; very little traffic was moving now because of Shabbat. He drove through the hills, his hills. Though he had been born in Lebanon, this was where he intended to live. He'd always have a job, too—killing Jews. He would hunt them down wherever they hid and end their miserable existence. But they were tough, he knew. They had outlived others who had tried to put an end to them. But that was before Abba. Killing came as naturally to him as breathing. He would never rest until every Jew had been wiped off the face of the earth. That was his mission. That was his reason for living.

There were those who would probably chastise him for leaving his troops at the Western Wall, but they simply didn't understand his mission. Allah had planned bigger things for him than dying at the hands of a crazy American. He had to live, to fulfill his purpose.

JAMIL ARMAN and Tomasso Metrano sat in the small office and watched the news reports on the portable black and white television. A young Israeli boy sat trembling beside them, stark fear in his wide eyes as he interpreted the Hebrew spoken by the newsman.

The boy spoke in a faltering voice, translating into English, which both men understood. "He says that men tried to blow up the *HaKotel* but did not succeed...."

Arman banged his fist on the desktop, the first time Metrano had seen the man lose his temper. "Go on," Arman growled.

"Eyewitnesses say that American men leading a small force shot the terrorists ... nearly fifty of them killed ... along with an American...."

"Tony," Metrano said, his fists clenching. Arman had managed to kill off his entire family.

"Your friend Bolan did this," Arman said. "If you had let Abba kill when—"

"Go to hell," Metrano said. "My boys are dead. All my boys, dead. I'm holding you responsible."

Arman shrugged without concern. "You are all a part of the glorious revolution," he said matter-of-factly. "They have given their lives for Islam. Allah will make a special place for them with many houri…"

"I don't care about your revolution!" Metrano said. "You have my children's blood on your hands."

Arman gazed at him through heavy-lidded eyes, then reached for an apple from a fruit basket. "Please, spare me the theatrics," he said, taking a bite of the apple. "Surely you have other sons…other wives.…"

"I'm no pervert!" Metrano said. "I'm a good Catholic, and I made this deal with you straightforward with no bullshit."

"We are partners sharing a common cause. Sometimes we must share common sorrow."

Big Tommy wanted to ice him right there, but he held back—waiting, wanting to have as much chance to escape as was possible under the awful circumstances.

The office door flew open, Abba standing there, his dark eyes smoldering.

"Well, I see *you* made it out okay," Metrano said, pointing a shaking finger. "Did you turn tail and run?"

"I have a duty here," Abba said, not even looking at Big Tommy. He pointed to the child. "Get the Jew out of here."

Arman remained silent, nodding to the boy who hurried to leave. Abba grabbed the child as he ran past, slapping him viciously about the face, then pushing him into the hall.

"Tough guy with little kids, aren't you, you bastard," Metrano said. "When the real men show up, you turn tail. Where's my Tony?"

Abba shrugged. "What's another American to me?"

Metrano jumped to his feet, throwing all his weight on the slight man. He pushed him up against the wall, the air going out of him. As he cocked a beefy fist to take out the bastard's nose, Arman spoke.

"That will be sufficient."

Big Tommy turned to see the man pointing an Uzi pistol at him. He glared at Arman, then released Abba, who slid to the floor, holding his stomach.

Then Abba pulled out the MR 73 and cocked the hammer.

"No," Arman said, turning the gun on Abba. "I will not permit any of that in here."

Abba glared darkly at him, then stood, holstering the pistol without a word. Arman set the automatic gently on the desktop.

"If you would kindly leave us," Arman told Metrano. "I have something to discuss with this man.

Our celebration is in the reception hall in thirty minutes."

"Yeah," Big Tommy replied. "You and me got some stuff to talk about, too."

"All in good time, my friend."

Metrano left, slamming the door behind him.

Abba moved closer to the desk as Arman reached out to shut off the sound on the television. "All of Israel has been broadcasting your failure and shame," Arman said.

Abba's lips tightened to a slash. "It wasn't my fault," he said.

"You were in charge," Arman replied. "The fault can be no one else's."

"That is not fair."

Arman laughed. "Fair is not a word to be applied to guerrilla fighters. There is only success . . . or failure."

"The circumstances were extremely difficult to work under," said Abba, talking quickly, nervously. "I shall succeed next time. I have had a great many ideas riding back here, I . . ."

Arman put up a hand to silence him, then took another bite from his apple, crunching loudly. "You are right in one thing," he said. "We will, indeed, do better next time. But next time, we will be doing it without you."

"What?"

"Your father is a very wealthy man, Abba," Arman said as he chewed. "He gave us a great deal of

money, and asked in return that we find a good place
for you in the organization. You kept getting in the
way here, so I sent you to America to wash you off of
me. But you just can't stop causing the wrong kind of
trouble, can you?''

"Please," Abba said. "I am a Palestinian, I will do
what..."

"You are a mad dog, Abba. And a coward on top
of that. There is no longer a place for you in our organization. It is only because of your father's money
that I let you live. Now get out. If I see you again, I
shall kill you."

Abba brought out the gun again, its long barrel
looking ridiculous in the closed-in office. His hand
was shaking slightly. "Suppose I kill you instead?"

Jamil Arman laughed loudly, a rumble that came
from deep in his huge stomach. "A formidable
weapon, to be sure," he said. "But something tells me
you won't kill me. You do not have the guts to face the
consequences. Now go, quickly. I can't stand the sight
of you."

Abba turned and strode from the office, walking
into the hot, moonless night. He'd go, all right, but
not before exacting his revenge on Jamil Arman. His
eyes fixed on the buildings holding the two hundred
hostages, the only thing that was keeping the Israel
army at bay. He felt his pockets for matches.

TOMASSO METRANO STOOD in his tiny bedroom and
stared at the grim faces of his seven remaining men.

They were all bound tightly to the Family, their loyalty solid. He felt a responsibility toward them.

"Tony's dead, too," he said, and put his hand up when the expressions of regret poured forth. "We'll have more than enough time to feel sorry later, but right now we've got to worry about gettin' out of this damned hellhole alive."

He walked to the bed and sat heavily. "I think that asshole, Arman, is tryin' to stiff us, too. First off, I want you to know that whatever money we come out of this thing with, we'll split even, all our shares equal."

Grunts of affirmation filled the room.

"But we got a lot to do first," Metrano said. "We got blood to be repaid, and we got a damned war zone to get out of. I got an idea to start with. Me and Arman and some of his soldiers are having a dinner in the reception hall in a few minutes. They won't really be expectin' nothin'. Now most of these bums are camped out at the perimeter. We need to take care of the ones left inside here, then maybe we can punch a hole through the damned fence or somethin' and get back over the border while we got the chance. You with me?"

The answer came back to Big Tommy loudly and enthusiastically. But, then again, what choice did any of them have?

28

Mack Bolan drove the coast highway, passing Haifa, then Acco as he moved inexorably toward Rosh Hanikra and the man who started all this. Johnny sat beside him, both men weary from two days of living hell, both pumping enough adrenaline to slide them through the confrontations yet to come.

The others followed in two cars, the big man's mission now their own. Bolan had confidence in his little force now. They had been honed to a cutting edge on a whetstone of horror and death.

Yeah, they were ready.

Five miles from the kibbutz, a government roadblock was turning back all traffic. Bolan pulled off the road well before the brightly lit blockade, the others parking behind him on the gravel shoulder. Everyone climbed out of the cars.

"The countryside isn't great," Bolan said, pointing off into the night, where the hills of Lebanon cast shadows in the distance, "but I think we can go overland. If we take all three cars, maybe one or two will get through."

"You lead," said a young bearded man named Moshe. "We'll follow."

Bolan nodded. "No lights," he said.

They climbed back into the vehicles. Bolan pulled his vehicle off the paved road and bounced onto pitted, hard-packed earth. He drove a half mile into the scrub brush, then turned north again, resuming the trek.

"How long do we stay off the roads?" Johnny asked.

"Until we can get past the roadblock."

"But what about the army? We'll run into them sooner or later."

"Right. We'll deal with them when we get there."

Johnny smiled at him across the expanse of darkness. "Just business as usual, huh?"

Bolan nodded. "You got it, brother."

One of the cars went into a ditch, breaking its front axle. The occupants split up into the two remaining cars. Once they had put sufficient distance between themselves and the roadblock, Bolan hurried back to the road, narrowing the gap between them and destiny.

It didn't take long. Thousands of troops were camped on the road ahead, with tents and portable buildings. Members of the news media roamed freely because it was one of the terrorist demands. There were trucks and tanks everywhere. Cars with the letters U.N. painted on them in black sat on the periphery of the activity. Bolan couldn't believe it. Civilian negotiators were involved, too.

And apart from it all, Bolan could see the PLO observation team, two men in black sitting in a jeep. They seemed to be in fine spirits, undoubtedly pumped up by all the uproar they had caused. They had fifty feet of free space around them in all directions.

As Bolan drove into camp, a whistle shrieked nearby. Within seconds the car was surrounded by uniformed troops, their faces grim, the Uzis they pointed at the Executioner itchy in their hands.

"I guess if you've got a plan," Johnny said, "now's the time to use it."

ABBA SET THE TIMER on the second incendiary bomb for one hour and started the clock mechanism. He smiled broadly, picturing Jewish bodies roasting in the fire storm of their dormitories when the bomb set off the wooden tinderboxes they were held in. But his greatest pleasure came in the thought of what would happen to Jamil Arman when the bombs went off. The troops would pour in, angry, seeking vengeance.

They all deserved to die, every one of them. Besides, with Arman out of the way, there would be no one to report Abba's failure to the organization. All would be as it had been, and his father would still love him.

He rose from his bed and stuffed the bombs in the small bag he had slung over his shoulder. He looked around the room to see if he had forgotten anything. A long stiletto that Tony Metrano had given him lay on a rough wooden desk.

He walked over and picked it up, the blade so narrow, so erotic. He had set the bombs for an hour. That would give him plenty of time to have a last friendly visit with one of the female prisoners, his blade doing most of the talking for him. Then he'd leave, crossing the border to await his next opportunity to enter his beloved Palestine.

So far, no one knew of his shame except for Arman. That would give him complete freedom of movement in camp. Good.

He left the room, moving swiftly through the wooden building and out into the night. He crossed the courtyard and approached the men's detention building. Very few guards maintained the camp interior; Arman wanted as many eyes on the perimeter as possible.

He moved to the building, pausing to converse for a moment with one of the guards there. Then, when the man had his back turned, he dropped one of the bombs on the ground and kicked it into the crawl space beneath the structure. Fifty-five minutes were left on the timer.

The building that housed the female captives was thirty feet away. Abba moved to it quickly, anxious now. His frustration levels were high—he needed an outlet.

He planted the bomb before rounding the corner of the building that housed the front entry. His friend, Irfan, was on duty there.

"Abba!" the man said, leaning his M-16 against the building. "I haven't seen you today."

"Important business," Abba returned. He pulled a package of cigarettes out of his pocket and shook one out for the man.

Irfan hesitated; Arman could sometimes be a stickler for Muslim custom. "Go ahead," Abba said impatiently. "No one will see you with the tobacco."

The man beamed. "Many thanks." He lit the smoke and drew on it, exhaling a long streamer.

"Is anyone in there?" Abba asked, thinking of Arman's ban on murdering the prisoners.

Irfan shook his head. "Broad daylight is the time for that," he said. "At night Arman wants us watching and relieving one another for sleep."

Abba smiled broadly. "I guess I shall have my pick then, eh?"

Irfan rolled his eyes and opened the door. "Tell them I send my love."

Abba moved into the dark recesses of the building—the prisoners weren't allowed lights at night. He took a small flashlight from his bag and shone it around. He was at the end of a long hallway, doors set on both sides, room after room of them. A flight of stairs was before him, the second floor above just like this one. He thought to go upstairs, better to muffle with distance any screams.

He climbed the steps, then walked the hall. About halfway down he began opening doors, shining his light on the frightened faces of the women in the rooms, moving along until he found what he was looking for.

He found her near the end of the hall, a blond woman, built large. His dark eyes danced as he moved into the room.

She said something to him in Hebrew that he didn't understand. Then in English she said, "Please leave. Please."

All the better. He walked up beside her, gently stroking her hair, her eyes shining, frightened in the darkness.

"It's going to be all right," he purred, then punched her hard in the jaw, knocking her flat on the bed. Twisting her long hair in his fist, he ripped her nightclothes off and fell upon her, enjoying her protests. He set the knife on the night table. He'd get to that later.

ALLIE YEAGER LAY IN BED and listened to the sounds of Shareen crying next door. The Arab was hurting her, she could tell that much, maybe killing her. This was a new direction, one that augured ill for all of them.

Shareen cried out loudly, in pain, and Allie sat up straight, putting her hands over her ears to try to shut out the sound. But she couldn't. She didn't need ears to hear inside her head what was going on.

She got out of bed, pacing the room. She walked back and forth, her mind whirling. She had to do something—and quickly.

Her pacing took her near the window. She glanced out by chance and saw a strange sight. Several of the American men, the Mafia she'd heard them called, were moving across the yard, their small group splintering off in all directions. They were moving their heads from side to side, looking all around. Something was happening.

Several of them disappeared from view, but her second-floor vantage point gave her a good view of many of them. She saw one coming toward her building. He walked up to the guard called Irfan and pulled a gun out of his pocket.

It went off silently. Irfan fell to the ground. The man grabbed the guard under the arms and pulled him into the building. She strained her eyes to see in the darkness. Another guard fell, then another.

The Mafia men moved quickly through the yard, disposing of the Arabs who guarded the women and the interior of the compound. Allie was frozen by several seconds of indecision, then a muffled scream from next door made up her mind for her.

They would never have a better chance to save their own lives than right here, right now. She thought of millions of Jews going off to German gas chambers without resistance. Then she thought of a handful of Jews holding off the whole German army for forty-two days in the Warsaw ghetto before escaping through the sewer systems.

"Never again," she whispered. "Never."

She quickly drew her clothes on and slipped out of her room. Moving quietly down the hall, she went from room to room, waking the others and preparing them to take their futures into their own hands again.

29

Mack and Johnny Bolan stepped out of the car with their hands in the air. "Nice day," Bolan said, hoping everyone here had been too busy with the current crisis to have seen his picture on television. Rough hands grabbed them, stripping their weapons, shoving them and the Sabras through the crowd toward an Israeli colonel who stood talking with a group of civilians.

The colonel, face drawn and pale, turned angrily toward them as they approached. *"Mah zeh?"* he said.

"I don't speak Hebrew," Bolan replied, putting his hands down and pushing away the Uzi barrel that was jamming him in the chest. "Are you in charge?"

"My name's Wolfson," the colonel said in English with a thick accent. "What do you want here?"

One of the civilians grabbed the colonel by the arm and spun him, completely ignoring Bolan. "What if we offered to trade some of your men for the same number of hostages? That would show our good faith."

"No, no," another man said angrily. "That would only make the problem permanent. I say, give them a deadline, then go in with the artillery if they don't meet it."

A tall, red-haired man laughed. "Will we take that on your authority, Isaac? Are you in charge of the military now?"

"I can't take orders from you," Wolfson told Isaac.

"Let's be realistic," the red-haired man said. "We haven't exhausted all the peaceful possibilities yet. I'm sure there must be a reasonable person in that kibbutz. Let's find him and negotiate."

"One of them committed suicide on command, to demonstrate their singlemindedness," Wolfson said. "They don't want to negotiate."

"Of course they want to negotiate," someone else said. "Everybody wants something. We just need to find out what it is they want."

"They want to kill us all," Wolfson said.

"Colonel," Bolan said curtly.

The officer turned back to Bolan, staring, while the civilians continued to argue among themselves.

Bolan met his stare. "I'm the man who saved the wall. I've got some ideas on this, but I'll need your help."

Wolfson just stared, his face rock-solid. "I'm up to my armpits in people with ideas," he said finally, spitting out the words. "I just don't have the time for you."

He looked at the soldiers holding Bolan's party. "Get them out of here," he said, turning back to the argument.

The Executioner pivoted quickly, planting an elbow in the stomach of the Israeli behind him. He grabbed the guy's Uzi and ran toward the terrorists, who sat, incredulous, in the jeep.

They were caught off guard, slow to react to Bolan's charge. They were still reaching for their weapons when the Executioner unleashed a couple of 3-shot bursts from the Israeli-made SMG.

He caught them both chest-high, the looks of surprise frozen on their faces as their lungs and hearts exploded under the impact. One of them fell out of the vehicle, the other collapsing across both seats.

Bolan swung around to face Wolfson across the open ground. The whole camp had stopped, everyone staring at him and what he had set in motion. Johnny was smiling broadly, nodding his head.

Bolan tilted the Uzi back on his shoulder and walked to Wolfson while people charged to the jeep. He stood in front of the man. "Now will you listen to me?" he said.

"You've just condemned those people to death," Wolfson said.

Bolan shook his head. "I can save them."

"Get on the phone," the red-haired man said. "We'll call them and ask their forgiveness, tell them a...crazy man did it."

"No," Isaac said. "They'll never believe it. Let's keep it quiet and bide our time for now."

"Oh, they'll handle that well," a tall man with a long-stemmed pipe said sarcastically.

Wolfson grimaced, then looked at Bolan. "What do you have in mind?" he asked.

Bolan pointed to the civilians. "Get rid of them, first off."

Wolfson looked from Bolan to the negotiators, then smiled. "Lieutenant Potock!" he called, and the man ran from the jeep to where they stood. "Both of them dead?"

The man nodded. "Yes, sir."

Wolfson grunted. "I want you to *escort* the negotiators back to their vehicles and safely beyond the roadblock. Don't let them back in." He put his hands on his hips and looked around the camp. "And get these damned reporters out of here, too."

"Yes, sir!"

Potock hurried to comply, everyone complaining loudly.

Bolan took the opportunity to retrieve his hardware and confer with Hillel, then he, Johnny and Colonel Wolfson walked to the jeep. "You've put my reputation on the line," the colonel said. "I hope you know what you're doing."

"My *life* will be on the line," Bolan said, pulling the body out of the jeep and onto the ground. "I'd better know what I'm doing." He patted Johnny on the shoulder. "This one looks about your size. Get into his clothes."

The Executioner began stripping the terrorist and putting on his clothes. "You speak their language?" he asked Wolfson.

The man nodded, his small mustache twitching. "I can get by."

"Good. There's a field phone in the jeep. Use it to call them up. Pretend you're one of these jokers. Tell them we're coming up with a message from the negotiating team."

"They'll be suspicious," Wolfson said.

"Of two men?" Bolan countered. "I don't think so."

"What will I do?" Wolfson asked.

"Get ready for the fireworks," the Executioner said. "When you hear shooting, move in with everything. The prisoners will be safe."

The two men exchanged looks, Bolan's even stare building Wolfson's confidence. The man made the call, speaking in Arabic. When he got off, he shrugged.

"No problem," he said.

Bolan had just finished dressing in the terrorist's blacks. He straightened and slung the dead man's M-16 over his shoulder, donning the man's olive-drab hat as an afterthought. "You know which buildings the hostages are in?" he asked.

Wolfson pulled a map out of his trouser pocket and pointed out the buildings. An aide hurried up to the jeep, saluting Wolfson. "Sir! The prime minister is calling. He wants to talk to you."

Wolfson folded up the map and gave it to Bolan. "Tell him I'm indisposed."

The aide's mouth fell open. "Sir, I..."

"Tell him, son," Wolfson said as he watched Bolan intently.

The aide ran off, Wolfson still watching Bolan. "I hope to God I see you again," he said, then pointed a finger. "I don't even know your name."

The Executioner climbed behind the wheel of the jeep, keying it to rattling life. "You just get your troops up there quick," he said, putting the machine in gear and lurching off.

TOMASSO METRANO WAS SO SICK of lamb, he thought he'd never wear another wool suit as long as he lived. He sat at the long banquet table, roast lamb piled in front of him on a platter, dripping fat. He'd had lamb for nearly every meal since coming to this damned country. There was rice also, and a great deal of fruit. To either side of him sat his chauffeur and his bodyguard, places of honor that were meant for Guido and Tony.

The thought of his sons made him stiffen with anger. But he kept it in check. He had learned to channel his anger many years before. It was an art form he was particularly well tuned for. He'd wait. Just a little while.

The table formed an L with another table. At this one sat Jamil Arman, resplendent in a white silk suit and white *ghutra*, plus eight of his officers, all dressed in what passed as uniforms in an illegal army.

The fat man was stuffing his face, grease glistening on his triple chin. Rings adorned every finger of both hands. Metrano looked at his watch. It was time to check the arrangements.

He scraped his chair back loudly, standing.

"Is something wrong?" Arman called to him, his face concerned.

"Naw," Metrano said. "I gotta go to the little boys' room."

The man looked at him quizzically.

"The water closet," Metrano said.

Arman nodded happily, returning to his food as Big Tommy made his way out of the narrow, long room.

He moved into the vestibule, ignoring the short hallway that led to the men's room. He opened the door to the outside.

One of his men, Angie, was waiting for him.

"Is it taken care of?" he asked.

The man nodded. "And we got a truck parked around back of this building."

Metrano nodded. "Good. Wait fifteen minutes. If there's any cash, we'll know by then. Go in and take care of the cooks, then come for me. We'll have to fight our way out of the banquet hall, but after that we can probably just drive out of the gate, free as the breeze."

Angie nodded and moved off into the darkness. Metrano spit on the doorstep and closed the door, walking back to the hall. Arman was dead, one way or the other, but if he did, indeed, have any money, it wouldn't hurt to take it out of there, too.

ABBA SMILED DOWN at the naked woman on the bed. Her face was battered and swollen, her blond hair matted with dried blood. Purple bruises covered her entire body. She moaned softly, clenching her teeth against the pain.

Abba moved to the night table, picking up the stiletto slowly, the woman following his movements with terrified eyes.

"Abba will give you an experience you'll never forget," he said in Arabic. "At least for the few minutes you have left."

He sat beside her on the bed and looked at his watch. He was running short on time himself. He needed to be out of there and gone in fifteen minutes.

"I am sorry I do not have the time to spend with you," he said. The woman forced herself to look at him. What she saw on her torturer's face was beyond the human imagination. She began to whisper a prayer in Hebrew.

He laid the point on her stomach gently, watching the slight indentation of the skin, the small trickle of blood right under the point. He wished he had set the timers for an hour and a half.

Suddenly a noise startled him; he turned to see a group of women coming into the room, one after another, five of them, ten, filling the small space.

"Get out of here!" he said in English. "Get out or you'll get the same!"

A searing pain in his wrist made him drop the knife. The woman on the bed had sat up and was biting his wrist, tearing a bloody section out of his arm.

He screamed, and the others descended on him, tearing at him with their hands and nails and teeth. Through waves of pain, he could feel his legs being forced apart....

30

"They're keeping it pretty dark," Johnny said, pointing to Rosh Hanikra, a half mile ahead.

"They don't want to be good targets," Bolan replied, gearing down to second to take a series of dips on the dirt road.

"You scared of this, Mack?" Johnny asked.

The Executioner smiled slightly. "I'd be crazy not to be. You?"

Johnny set his jaw. "Yeah. A bit. But I'm not worried about it."

"It all depends on the gate. If they open it before we get there, we're okay. If not, we lose it on the spot."

Johnny shook his head. "*Now* I'm worried about it."

"Here we go," Bolan said, the kibbutz looming large in their vision. Soldiers were everywhere, fanned out around the fenced perimeter.

"It's a whole army," Johnny said. "There's hundreds of them."

"And they've got cars pulled in front of the gate. Quick, stand and start waving your arms for them to move the cars."

Johnny stood, as his brother jammed on the horn, both of them yelling and gesticulating wildly with their arms. They were approaching the gate at thirty miles per hour, a quick enough flash that no one could tell who they were. But if they had to stop, they'd never get in.

The gate was fifty yards away, forty. Bolan slowed to twenty-five, but they had mere seconds left before—

They were in the midst of the terrorist army, men running out of their path, diving for cover. All at once, the curtain of cars parted and they zipped through without slowing, just barely missing the fender of a truck. Someone was yelling at them in Arabic, pointing to a one-story building off to the side of the main cluster of structures.

"What's he want?" Johnny said.

"I'll bet that's where our boy is," the Executioner answered, as he tried to cover his face from the lines of troops blurring past. Then, all at once, they were through the congestion onto open, clear ground. There wasn't a uniform in sight.

Johnny turned around to see the cars close up the opening again. "Doesn't make sense that there aren't any troops in this part of the compound."

Bolan shook his head, steering the car toward the building the man pointed out. "Something's not right," he said.

The Executioner drove up close to the building, turning off his lights. Then he circled, taking note of a deuce and a half parked behind the place, and took off toward the dormitories where the hostages were being held.

"You ready?" he asked his brother.

"What do you think?" Johnny replied, as he checked the silencer on his MAC-10.

They pulled into the shadows of the men's dormitory, and shut off the engine. It was deathly quiet as they slipped from the vehicle and moved up to flatten themselves against the structure.

"The prisoners would be under guard, wouldn't they?" Johnny whispered.

Bolan shrugged, pointing to a door at the far end of the dorm.

They crept toward the entry, hugging the shadows. The door stood ajar, two boots visible in the spill of light from outside.

Eyes searching the night, Bolan hoisted himself up the stairs and into the building, passing a dead terrorist stretched out in the vestibule.

Johnny was up seconds later. "There's a dead man stuffed under the building..." he began, eyebrows jumping when he saw the one inside. "What in the hell is going on here?"

"Somebody's doing our job for us," Bolan said, moving through the entry to the hallway. Men were peeking out of their doors in the darkness, some of them moving into the hall.

"*Shalom,*" Bolan whispered harshly into the dark. "We're here to help you."

A crowd ran to greet them, others hurrying down the stairs. They were all dressed, ready to go.

"Did you kill the guards?" the Executioner asked.

"No," a man said. "We saw them that way. We thought you did it."

"Never mind," the nightfighter said. "Just be prepared. We're going to the women's building, then we're getting out of here. The enemy are defending the perimeter, but most of them are jammed up by the front gates. My men will be there to help us where the back fences run into the hills in the southwest corner."

"We'll be ready," a man said with determination, the others assenting firmly.

The two Bolans moved quickly out of the dorm, running the distance to the women's prison. They found two more dead terrorists on the way, and another in the entry hall of the building.

Like the men in the other dorm, women were milling about in the hall. "Round them up," Bolan said, running up the steps to the second floor. "I'll get the ones up here."

He made the second landing; some sort of commotion was going on at the end of the hall. He ran toward it, urging the female prisoners downstairs as he passed them.

About twenty women were crowded around one of the last rooms. "Whoever wants to get out of here, come with me," he said. "Come on ladies, hurry!"

They began filing out quickly, many of them covered with blood. Within seconds, the Executioner was alone with what was left of Abba.

The man lay naked on the bed, horribly mutilated. Flesh was pulled away exposing bone. One of his eyes had been poked through, blood and fluid oozing down his raw cheeks. Teeth were nothing but jagged stumps, bloody froth bubbling from the remnants of his lips. Bones were broken, his limbs twisted at ridiculous angles from his body. Barely an inch of his skin was untouched.

And he was still alive, his one good eye wide in horror, jerking back and forth.

The Executioner heard footsteps running down the hall. Then his brother's voice was calling him. "Mack...everyone's downstairs, I..."

Johnny came around the doorframe and saw Abba. He walked in slowly, his face an unreadable mask.

The man was trying to speak, his words liquid with his own blood. "P-Please...kill...me."

The brothers shared a look, then Bolan reached out a hand and put it on Johnny's shoulder. "I'll be downstairs," he said.

A heartbeat later, Bolan heard a single shot.

31

Mack and Johnny Bolan moved swiftly, covering the distance between the dorms and the banquet hall. Their hands were filled with silenced automatics, their minds locked onto the completion of their mission.

The hostages waited by their prisons for the big man to lead them to freedom, and that was certainly his main responsibility; but there was something else that had to be done first.

Loose ends.

They reached the wooden structure and flattened themselves against it. The windows were all heavily draped.

"I can hear voices inside," Johnny said, ear to the wall.

The Executioner nodded, the Ingram in his right hand, the Linda in his left. "Let's get this over with," he said.

They charged around to the front door, positioning themselves on either side. Bolan nodded to his brother and they kicked the door wide, diving and rolling inside.

Mafia buttons filled the vestibule. Minds elsewhere, they swung around in surprise, five of them, and the Executioners opened up. The execution was swift and merciless.

Within seconds the hardmen lay in a heap on the floor, limbs twisted and faces grotesque and strained. Their blood ran down the walls and splotched the furniture.

The savages hadn't time to fire a single shot.

Bolan and Johnny uncurled immediately, standing to reload quickly. Loud voices drew them to the banquet room.

TOMASSO METRANO GLANCED at his watch. It was time to start things rolling, if only Arman would shut up and get on with it.

The fat man was standing, gesturing expansively to everyone in the room. "Let this be the moment that ushers in a close and eternal relationship between our two families. We have joined in a glorious revolution together under the eyes of Allah, and even now, we stand at the threshold of our new nation, our foothold secure...."

"I hate to interrupt," Big Tommy said loudly, "but don't you think I've waited long enough to get paid for my end of our little relationship? I swear to God, Jamil, you could talk me to death before I finish dessert."

One of Arman's lieutenants stood up, eyes flashing. "Silence! You cannot talk like this. Where is your respect?"

"I respect the dollar, chump," Metrano said, sick of the game. "That lard bucket you call a leader gets nothin' but a laugh out of me."

Arman was livid, his face reddening with every word. "How can you insult my honor this way?" he said loudly. "You have shamed me in front of my own people!"

"Go to hell, pig," Metrano said, standing. "I want my money and I want it right now. If you got it, put it up on the table. If not, I'll take it out of your ass."

Arman's people were coming to their feet, hands reaching for weapons. Arman put his hands out, motioning them back to their seats.

"So, it is only the filthy money you want," he said, bending down to reach under the table. He drew out a large aluminum suitcase and set it on the table. "I'll give you your money, and you can spend it in hell."

"I don't think so," came a voice from the entry.

They turned to see the Executioner standing before them, Johnny at his side. Two of the uniformed troops standing by the wall went for their guns. Bolan turned the Linda on them, taking them out without moving his eyes from Big Tommy.

Everyone else stopped, watching the big man. The Bolans moved farther into the room and stood, weapons ready, before the tables.

The Executioner glared at Big Tommy, who returned his glare in full measure. "I've been looking for you," he said.

Big Tommy spit on the ground. "So you found me. What am I supposed to be, impressed?"

"Money," Arman said. "I will give you all the money you can use. Do what you want with him, but I'll give you ten million dollars to leave me alone. I'll protect you and get you out of the country."

The Executioner turned to look at the man. He opened the suitcase. It was jammed full of hundred-dollar bills.

"I'll be damned," Big Tommy said in surprise.

"See?" Arman said. "Kill him, I don't care. Then take this. You'll be rich, free to live out your life as you choose."

Mack Bolan never even looked at the case. Instead, he squeezed off a short burst, blasting through the top of the suitcase, money flying into the air to float gently to the ground.

Arman backed away from the suitcase, several large holes punched through his huge stomach. His hands were shaking in front of him as blood squirted, drenching his white suit.

He looked surprised, as if he was wondering why the feeling hadn't soaked through his immense bulk to reach his brain yet.

Without a word, he stumbled backward, banging the wall, knocking his black rimmed glasses askew on his face. Then, like a mechanical man, he came forward again and pitched across the table, falling into a large plate full of lamb, blood staining the white tablecloth.

Bolan turned back to Metrano.

"You ain't gonna get no satisfaction out of me," Big Tommy said.

"No," Bolan replied. "Only the knowledge that you won't take up the space meant for decent people."

"You ain't no different than me," Metrano spat.

"That's where you're wrong," Bolan said, as he and Johnny opened up on the whole tableful of them.

Twelve people jerked in their seats, many of them trying to fire back. Parabellum slugs devoured people, table, chairs and all, the suitcase jumping on the table, sending money flying everywhere. Metrano was screaming, cursing loudly as the slugs tore at his chest.

Everyone was down except Metrano, who stumbled like a sleepwalker, arms stiff in front of him. He had pulled out one of his pearl-handled guns and carried it loosely, by the barrel. He tried to walk out, weaving crazily, then simply keeled over, the breath going out of him in a long, wheezing gasp.

But the Executioner wasn't even there for his end. He and Johnny were already off, charging around the back of the banquet hall for the truck they had seen earlier.

They climbed into the vehicle, Bolan behind the wheel. The engine hesitated, turning over slowly, then finally ground to life.

"Let's get out of here," Johnny said.

As they crossed the yard, some of the troops were drifting back to the building complex. Johnny laid the Ingram on the windowsill and emptied the clip, four men going down amid a shower of dust.

They reached the women's building, pulling around to the back where they crouched in shadows.

"Fill the truck, quickly!" Bolan said. "Let's go. The rest of you on foot."

Within twenty seconds, they were moving toward the men's building, while other troops from the perimeter rushed back toward the complex.

As the truck reached the male quarters, the women's exploded in a huge fireball, Abba's incendiary grenade going up under the structure. The whole area was now daylight-bright.

"This is it!" Bolan yelled. "Come on!"

He pulled away from the building, people clustering around the truck and running behind it. Troops were charging toward them, firing, but still at a distance.

"It's up to Wolfson now," the Executioner said, and the men's building exploded, twin conflagrations reaching fifty feet into the night sky.

They raced across the grounds toward the point of least resistance. Terrorist troops pulled away from the fences to block their escape as Wolfson's men charged the kibbutz.

The battle was met. The terrorists were good targets under the glaring firelight, grenades exploding in their midst, 50-caliber machine guns thinning their ranks. But they were still formidable. Johnny leaned out of the window to give them a taste of the Ingram, as incoming fire shattered the windshields.

Then the Sabra group pitched in. They had silently infiltrated the area, almost to the battle lines. When they stood and began firing at the unprotected backs of the terrorists, they were no more than twenty feet from the fence.

The terrorists turned to defend their flanks, and Bolan plowed right through them in the truck. Men flew in all directions, several of them being ground under the wheels as the truck plunged through the fence, and broke free to the other side.

The Israelis ran, cheering, through the broken place, seeking safety in the night. But the PLO mob was no longer interested in anything but trying to protect their own hides.

Once Bolan saw that the Israeli hostages were clear, he pulled a one-eighty and drove back into the action.

Johnny raked any surviving terrorists who crossed their path.

Within five minutes it was all over. Bolan finally stopped the truck at the edge of an apple orchard. He and Johnny climbed down.

"Did we lose any of the hostages?" he asked his brother.

Johnny smiled. "Not one," he said.

They picked their way through the yard, which was now littered with Arab bodies. The Israelis were mourning their own dead, medics rushing frantically around with stretchers to provide aid for the wounded.

Ambulance sirens could be heard continuously. But the Israeli casualties seemed small, no comparison to the PLO dead. It looked, on surface at least, that the operation had been a resounding success.

This fact did not surprise the Executioner nor his brother. They understood this kind of warfare.

Wolfson found them in the confusion. "The hostages are safe," he said, his expression, as always, unreadable. "I don't know who you are, but I doubt if it will be safe for you around here."

Bolan nodded. "I know."

The colonel reached out and shook their hands, the action telling more than mere words ever would. "Is there anything I can do for you?" he asked.

Bolan nodded. "Give us a jeep and an hour's head start."

"Done," Wolfson said, and handed them a set of keys. "It's parked next to my command post."

Bolan took the keys. "Live large," he said.

Wolfson watched the two warriors turn and stride back into the night.

And it occurred to the colonel that he still hadn't learned their names. It bothered him as he stood staring into the gloom, wondering about the apparition in black who had delivered his people from the forces of evil. Did he imagine it? Did this wraith of death have a name?

Yes, he did. From the slime-infested back alleys of America to the corrupt streets of Europe and the hellholes of Iran and Afghanistan, all the way to the Kremlin itself, death had a name. It was Mack Bolan.

You don't know what
NONSTOP
HIGH-VOLTAGE
ACTION
is until
you've read your
4 FREE
GOLD EAGLE
NOVELS

LIMITED-TIME OFFER

Mail to Gold Eagle Reader Service

In the U.S.
P.O. Box 1396
Buffalo, N.Y. 14240-1396

In Canada
P.O. Box 609
Fort Erie, Ont.
L2A 9Z9

YEAH! Rush me 4 free Gold Eagle novels and my free mystery
bonus. Then send me 6 brand-new novels every other month as
they come off the presses. Bill me at the low price of just $14.95—
a 13% saving off the retail price. There are no shipping, handling or
other hidden costs. There is no minimum number of books I must
buy. I can always return a shipment and cancel at any time. Even if
I never buy another book from Gold Eagle, the 4 free novels and the
mystery bonus are mine to keep forever.　　166-BPM-BP6F

Name　　　　　　　　　(PLEASE PRINT)

Address　　　　　　　　　　　　　　　　Apt. No.

City　　　　　　　State/Prov.　　　　Zip/Postal Code

Signature (If under 18, parent or guardian must sign)

This offer is limited to one order per household and
not valid to present subscribers. Price is
subject to change.

MYSTERY BONUS GIFT

HV-SUB-1-RRR